Smile Time Books are written for anyone who enjoys a feel-good story, and their short chapters make them ideal for reading to children at bedtime.

Other books by Robert Kingsley Hawes

The Girl I the Yellow Hat
The Jetty War

A Dog on the Run

The Magpie Way (book 1)
Finding Alice

When Pop Took Us Fishing

My 13-year-old grandnephew, who is also my namesake, offered to do some sketches for this book. Naturally, I asked his mother for approval as I did not want to interfere with his homework, but the question was irrelevant. It appears that I take longer to drink a cup of coffee than he takes to do a sketch. Thank you, Robert Hawes the second, for your contribution to this book.

THE MAGPIE WAY

The Great River

Robert Kingsley Hawes

Published by Smile Time

ISBN 978-0-6452189-2-3 (paperback)

Illustrations by Robert Russell Hawes

First edition, 2022

For book orders and enquiries, contact: r.hawes70@gmail.com

A catalogue record for this book is available from the National Library of Australia

CONTENTS

CONTENTS

1

A NEW BEGINNING

Max opened an eye and peeped out. In the distance was the first glow of dawn. A new day was coming, and he needed to be awake, for Magpies were Mother Nature's chosen creatures. It was their duty to herald the sun, but Max's body ached. His journey from the city had taken its toll, and he thought Mother Nature might excuse him that morning. He closed both eyes again.

Max was finding it hard to believe that his sister had chosen to live so far from family. Their parents, Grandma, and Aunty Jenny were all back home in Gum Tree Park. Mayzie, who was Max's girlfriend, was back there too. He had left them all behind when he left home to find his sister.

Max had come across Brian who was their brother, not long after leaving home. Brian had been a bully to his siblings but was their father's favourite son. Their father thought that Max would always fail, while Brian was destined to become a leader. But Max had found him living in a wildlife park and Brian was now afraid of the outside world.

Alice, who was Max's sister, had left home when her father tried to kill her, while Max left after having a brutal fight with him. 'Go find your sister,' were the last words Max heard his mother say.

Max knew that Alice would try to find the mythical Great River, for a wise Koala named Nebbie had told her that was where Mother Nature's creatures gathered to exchange wisdom and knowledge.

Alice never did find the river, but her plan helped Max find her. She was living on a small farm in the middle of nowhere and had become the companion of a boy named Colin, who spent most of his time in a wheelchair.

Max thought it would take a miracle to mend the bad things that had torn their family apart. His duty now, was to stay with his sister, for she was the only Magpie living in that part of the world.

***

Alice jabbed Max in the ribs, bringing an end to his doze. 'Wake up, sleepy head. We have to welcome the sun.'

Max clenched his eyes tight, hoping she would go elsewhere to perform their Magpie duty, but she pulled a feather in his tail. He nearly fell out of the tree. 'Ouch,' he squawked. 'I nearly fell thanks to you.'

'Sorry,' said Alice. 'Perhaps you should be wearing a parachute.'

'Magpies don't wear parachutes.'

'They don't normally fall out of trees either,' giggled Alice.

Max frowned. He had never won an argument with his sister. He blinked, stretched his wings, and shook his feathers. His sister would let him sleep no more, and so they welcomed the sun with a duet of Magpie carolling. It was then time for breakfast and Adam's vegetable garden beckoned.

The vegetable garden was a place of every Magpie's dream, a happy hunting ground where tasty creatures lurked everywhere. They could be found sheltering among the vegetables or under every sod of dirt.

Adam was Colin's dad and Evelyn was his mum, and they called their farm Eden Springs. *I think I could enjoy living here,* thought Max as he scoffed his fourth grub, but his grandma had a saying. *Nothing stays the same forever.* Alas, wise old grandma was about to be proven right.

'Max, you can't stay here,' said Alice, who could tell what Max was thinking.

Max ignored Alice's remark. *Girls always like to spoil things,* he thought.

'You can't stay here,' she repeated.

'Why?'

'This is not the life for you. Colin has adopted me as a member of his family, but you need a flock to live with.'

'So do you,' Max reasoned.

'Perhaps, but it is more important that I stay here and make Colin happy.'

Max was surprised to hear that Alice would sacrifice her Magpie way of life in favour of keeping a Human happy. She had set out to find wisdom and knowledge at the Great River but appeared to have given up on her dream.

Alice repeated herself for a third time. 'You can't stay here. I avoid the Crows, but you will want to fight them, and you can't spend your life fighting Crows.'

Max had alarmed Alice the previous day when several Crows had come for a visit. He could not tolerate their presence, for Crows had twice plotted to kill him.

'You can help me fight the Crows,' he replied.

'No, because that would be futile. It would take more than two Magpies to keep the Crows away. If you stay, you will be fighting them on your own.'

Alice was right. Max hated Crows, and he was too proud to tolerate their taunts. But his dilemma was interrupted by a voice.

'Good morning, Alice.'

An Emu was standing at the fence that protected Adam's lettuces from the ravages of Rabbits. She had several chicks with her, all peering through the wire netting.

'Good morning, Giselle. This is my brother, Max.'

Max had hoped to meet an Emu because Alice had told him that the farm's Sheep called each other Bruce. This seemed a strange coincidence, for he had met an Emu called Lofty who had a Sheep friend called Garry, but Lofty called his friend Bruce.

'Good morning, Giselle,' he said. 'You wouldn't happen to know if an Emu called Lofty comes from these parts?'

Giselle was taken aback, and she stammered, 'Lofty is my boy. We lost him a good while ago.'

Max had often thought about becoming a detective, and suddenly he had a case to solve. Was the Lofty being held as a prisoner in the graveyard of the Church of Nowhere, Giselle's son. 'What happened to Lofty?' he asked.

Giselle told how Lofty had been the fastest runner in the mob, but he never looked where he was going. He had tripped, hitting his head when some Humans chased him. Last ever seen of him, was his lifeless body being thrown into the back of a ute.

Max had his suspicions but said nothing. He did not want to give a mother false hope, but he now had two people needing help. Alice needed to be in a flock and Giselle needed to know what happened to her son.

In the rashness of youth, he made a snap decision and turned to Alice. 'You are right,' he said. 'I cannot live here without a flock, but neither can you, so I am going back to get one.'

RETURNING HOME

Max would face many obstacles on the trip home, but none greater than the waterless, Mallee Plain. This he would face on the first day, a perilous crossing that had almost taken his life the last time he did it. On the far side of the plain was a low range of hills, and that was where he would find water at a place the Pigeons called the Wilderness Windmill. That was where he had met a Pigeon called Homer who had told him how to get to the Great River.

Annoyingly, he would pass another windmill on the way, but it was guarded by Crows. This band of cut-throats drove all birds away, hoping they would die of thirst. Max was one of the few to survive their evil plan, but he would need a cool day if he were to bypass their windmill again.

He waited for a cool day but was in no hurry to leave. He was enjoying life at Eden Springs, despite an occasional visit by Crows. Alice had given him strict orders to keep the peace, but she could see that Max's willpower was fading. A Max versus Crows war was inevitable.

Finally, a cool day came, but Max pretended not to notice. It was Alice who said, 'Okay, Max, time to leave.'

He did not argue, for he thought it normal for an older sister to be the bossy one, even though they were born at almost the same time. It also came as no surprise when Alice gave him a long lecture, telling him to make sure that he stayed safe.

With lecture given, Max said goodbye and headed for the hills. He recalled that the windmill stood at a place where the hills took a dip, and he could see that dip in the distance. However, it was only when he got closer that he saw the actual windmill. This sighting came as a great relief. He had passed his first test in navigation, but many more were to come.

That night, he rested at the windmill, which he greeted like a long-lost friend. Some may wonder how a Magpie could consider a windmill to be a friend, but it had been Max's sole companion during the many days he had been stranded at the edge of the Mallee Plain. This steadfast contraption gave more than lifesaving water. In Max's mind, it became a lonely monster, stranded on the edge of nowhere and speaking to him through the endless groan of its pump.

Next morning, he farewelled his isolated friend and set out on what would be another thirsty day. His plan was to reach the Lookout by nightfall. This prominent landmark lay on the far side of a stretch of barren hills, but failure to find it would see him lost in those hills, a place where no Magpie could survive for long. Another day of perfect navigation was needed.

Max was relying on the sun to guide him that second day. Previously, he had crossed the hills by flying toward the place from where it rises. For the return journey, he flew to where it sets, and the sun did not let him down.

Max reached the Lookout by nightfall but did not go close, for it was home to the Great Gandor, an Eagle that feasted on creatures Max's size. He took this precaution despite the Eagle being a friend, for he could not risk being mistaken for a stranger in the half light of evening. It was one of the many warnings included in Alice's lecture.

That evening, he scanned the sky, hoping to see the beacon that would guide him home. A Blue-wren had told him how the sky glows above the city at night and Max was hoping to see that glow, but at first, he saw nothing. He continued scanning as the sky darkened, all the time wondering what to do should he not see the glow. Then, when all evidence of the sunset was gone, he saw it in the distance.

Max could rest at last, and as he dozed, he thought about Tinka and Tinkalina, the tiny Blue-wrens who had told him about the glow. He owed them so much, for they were the first to show Alice kindness when she fled home, and they were equally as kind when he came upon them. On that occasion, Tinka could see that the Crows were plotting to kill him, and he stepped in and saved Max's life. Max wondered if he had thanked them properly and resolved to pay them a visit before reaching home.

The next day saw Max in greener pastures. He was still flying over hills, but it was farmland, where the Humans had carved paddocks into a once natural landscape of trees and bushes. He thought about visiting Brian, who lived in the Well-Meaning Wildlife Park, but he did not want to risk a detour.

It took another day for Max to reach the highway that led to the city. This was a familiar trail he could follow, and he soon found himself at the graveyard behind the Church of Nowhere. He landed on the statue of the angel, which was the tombstone Max could never fathom. He had been brought up to believe that birds were superior to Humans, because Humans could not fly, but here was a statue of a Human with wings.

He looked around and saw Lofty at the graveyard fence, looking out as he waited for Garry to pay him his regular visit. Lofty turned and saw Max. 'Hi, Max,' he said.

'Lofty, you remember my name.'

'How could I forget your name?' asked Lofty.

'But Lofty, you are the world's most forgetful Emu. You are not supposed to remember anything,' said Max.

'I am?' said Lofty.

'You are,' said Max.

'I are what,' asked Lofty.

'You are the world's most forgetful Emu.'

Lofty frowned. 'Max, if anyone had told me that, I would remember.'

'I just did tell you that,' said Max.

'You did just tell me what?' asked Lofty.

Max shook his head. There were two people in the world he was never going to win an argument with. One was his sister, and the other was Lofty, but at least Alice's arguments made sense.

As Lofty came closer, a twinkle came to his eye. 'I think my friend likes you sitting on her,' he said.

The flying Human is your friend?' asked Max.

'Yes, I talk to her all the time. She keeps me company.'

'But she is made of stone.'

Lofty shrugged, and then his eyes resumed their faraway glaze. There was no point in further discussing the flying Human.

Max smiled to himself. Who was he to pass judgement on someone who has a stone statue as a friend? Two days before, he had been having similar conversations with his good friend, the Wilderness Windmill. Lofty and he had more things in common than he previously realised.

'What is your mother's name?' Max asked.

'Giselle,' came the reply.

Max's eyes gleamed. His hunch was correct. Detective Max had solved the case, and what was needed now, was a plan to reunite mother and son. He had some ideas but said no more, for his plan still needed work. He said goodbye and continued along the highway. Next stop would be the home of Tinka and Tinkalina.

Max landed in the Blue-wren's clearing expecting to hear their tweets, but there was only silence. Concerned, he looked about. The wrens were so tiny and defenceless. Something bad could have happened. He began thinking the worst, but they were simply being cautious. After carefully assessing their visitor, they appeared and began hopping around, each trying to out-tweet the other.

'Hi Max, great to see you,' tweeted Tinker.

'Hello, Max. Wonderful to see you again,' tweeted Tinkalina. 'Did you find Alice?'

'Hello to you both,' Max warbled, 'and yes, I did find Alice. She is living in a place called Eden Springs.'

Tinkalina began a greeting song, causing Max to recall the last time they met. He was sometimes insensitive to the feelings of others, and on that occasion, he had upset her. He needed to make amends. 'You are looking very nice today,' he complimented.

'Thank you,' she tweeted. 'I am feeling much better now that my migraines have gone, and I am so glad to hear that you found Alice.'

Tinker interrupted. 'Tinkalina is much happier now her migraines are gone.'

Max expected Tinker to be in trouble for interrupting his wife, for Tinka was the most hen-pecked husband Max had ever met, but Max was wrong. Tinkalina gave her husband a look of approval. 'Tinker is so kind the way he looks after me when I'm not well,' she said.

What a difference her migraines make, Max mused to himself.

He stayed with the wrens that night, listening to Tinkalina as she carried on about clouds, rainbows, stars, and noisy trucks. Her enthusiasm for life gave new meaning to these everyday things. Meanwhile, her husband perched in silence, content that his wife was feeling well again.

Next day, Max travelled on to the gorge and stayed the night, for the gorge was like no other place he had ever known. It was the highlight of his journey. Sometimes, he would tell others of its tranquil beauty, its aromas, its symphony of sounds, and the feeling you got by being there, but he could never put it into words. 'It is something you just have to experience for yourself,' he would say to them.

Home was now only a day away, but Max felt in no hurry to get there. The gorge was beckoning him to stay, but duty was telling him otherwise. He had made a promise to his sister which he intended to fulfil.

3

NOTHING STAYS THE SAME FOREVER

Next morning, Max reached the end of the gorge beyond which lay suburbia, but he knew his way home from there. The creek that flowed through the gorge was the same that flowed past the tree where he was born. He only had to follow it.

His journey ended in the late afternoon when he landed on the seat in the middle of Gum Tree Park. There he perched on the object that brought back so many childhood memories, but then realised that his father would soon be aware of his return. He was tired from his journey and not ready for another fight. *Perhaps I should have stayed away until morning,* he thought, but it was already too late.

His father was nowhere to be seen, but his mother saw him arrive. She flew down and fussed excitedly, saying how wonderful it was to have him back. Then she took a closer look. 'You are looking a bit thin,' she said. 'You need to tidy yourself up before people see you.'

Grandma heard the commotion and swooped in to join them. She expressed her delight to see Max, and then said, 'Your mother is right. You should tidy yourself up. That nice Mayzie girl is still around, and she doesn't have a bloke yet. You two are made for each other, but you won't impress her looking scruffy.'

Why can't mothers and grandmas leave it at, 'Hello Max'? Max thought. He continued looking around but did not ask about his father, for he did not want people to think that he still cared about or feared him.

That night, he ate a hearty meal, thinking that it might improve his waistline. Then he preened his feathers, having first made sure that no one was watching. He was taking Grandma's advice, for he wanted to make a good impression on Mayzie, but he did not want people to know.

Still worried about his appearance, he decided to avoid the meeting tree next day, thinking Mayzie might be there. He wanted to put on more weight before seeing her, and so went looking for his other friends instead.

First to be found was his former tutor, Nebbie. As expected, he was asleep in a nearby tree. 'Wake up, Nebbie, I'm back,' squawked Max.

Max liked waking Nebbie, for his friend's grumpy reaction always amused him, but this time was different. Nebbie was delighted to see the return of his former pupil, and he broke into an unexpected smile. Then he listened with interest as Max told him about finding Alice, and about meeting the Great Gandor. Nebbie had warned them not to visit this legendary monarch of the bush for he always ate his visitors. 'You were lucky not to get eaten,' he said, and Max agreed.

Max went on to tell his other stories and it was soon apparent that Nebbie was now the pupil and Max was the teacher. Nebbie had often talked about the Great River but thought it belonged in the realm of mythology. When Max told him he knew how to get there, Nebbie sat speechless.

Max asked Nebbie for a scientific explanation for the strange things he had seen on his journey, but Gum Tree Park's resident scientist just shook his head. 'You have a very curious mind, young Max,' he said. 'You should consider becoming a scientist and not a detective. You could be the first to discover the scientific reasons for the strange things you have seen, and you would be famous.'

Max was disappointed that Nebbie could not answer his questions, but becoming famous had appeal. Perhaps he could do it all. An adventure seeking detective could journey to the Great River and solve scientific mysteries in his spare time.

'I should think about that,' said Max, but Nebbie did not answer. He had dropped off to sleep, which was how Nebbie's conversations usually ended.

Next on Max's list was Dopey. He had never gotten on with this odd-ball Dove, but Dopey had taught Alice the dove-dive, the trick that had saved her from becoming Great Gandor food. *Where is that crazy*

Dove? he thought as he searched in vain. Finally, the meeting tree was the only place left to look.

The meeting tree was the secret place where Alice and Dopey could meet without being discovered by Alice's father. It was also the place where Max would meet Mayzie, which was the reason he was currently avoiding it.

He landed in the tree, and sure enough, there was Mayzie. Dopey, on the other hand, was conspicuous by his absence. *That rotten Dopey is always messing things up for me,* Max thought, but Mayzie was delighted to see the return of her long-lost hero.

'Hello, Max, you look great!' Her voice was full of excitement.

I sure don't understand girls, thought Max. His mother had told him that he looked terrible.

'Hi, Mayzie. You look great, too.'

Max hoped that he had just said the right thing, for he had a habit of putting his foot in it. He had missed Mayzie but was not sure how to tell her. He was shy when it came to showing his feelings, and so he told her about Eden Springs and its excellent trees for nest building. Then he told her about his mission to recruit a flock, and finally he said how nice it would be if she could come with him to Eden Springs.

'Are you proposing?' Mayzie asked, coyly.

'You mean like getting married?' Max mumbled.

'That's what I mean.'

'Well, I guess—'

At that moment, Dopey landed on the branch.

'Hi, Dopey.' Max and I are getting married,' announced Mayzie. 'Would you like to be the first to congratulate us?'

Dopey slapped a wing on Max's back. 'Well done, buddy. Congratulations. How has all this come about?'

Max was still wondering the same thing. He did want to marry Mayzie but thought that proposals were done in a more romantic setting. *Did I just propose, and did she just accept?* he wondered. 'I'm not sure, Dopey,' he answered, but he was happy how it had all turned out.

'Did you hear about your old man?' Dopey asked.

'No,' replied Max, 'I've been wondering why no one is talking about him. I guess he will come looking for me soon.'

Dopey laughed. 'No worries there. The Humans took him prisoner.'

'Is this true?' Max asked Mayzie.

'Yes,' she said. 'They caught him in a net and took him away in a cage.'

Mazie hoped that Max would not be upset, but to everyone's surprise, he was. His dad had many faults, but he was still his dad. He would have been happy for his dad's faults to disappear, but not at the cost of his dad disappearing along with them. He changed the subject, as a way of hiding his feelings, and told them about Alice.

'Did you give Alice my message?' Dopey asked.

'Sorry, I forgot. I will tell her when I get back.'

'One message, I give you one message; one message, and you forget.' Dopey was annoyed.

'Not everything is about you, Dopey. We had a lot going on.' Max was trying not to laugh.

'One message, it was only one message. There are no excuses.'

'Yes, I did tell her,' Max finally admitted, 'but she said to tell you that she already knew that she was not a scaredy-cat.'

'You have a warped sense of humour,' Dopey snorted. He turned his back and flew off in a huff.

'That was a bit mean,' said Mayzie. 'You could have told him all that in the first place.'

'Just getting even,' Max laughed.

The newly engaged couple spent the rest of the day visiting all their favourite places, but without the worry of Max's dad seeing them. Things were different than before. His dad was gone, and Mayzie was planning their wedding. Wise old grandma's saying was holding true. Nothing stays the same forever.

4

FREEDOM

Charlie the Cockatoo was last on Max's visiting list, for he thought that Charlie would be annoyed with him. He had left on his journey without saying goodbye, and he had no excuse for what he had done. He owed his friend an apology, which was something he had been putting off.

It was late that afternoon, that he landed in front of Charlie's cage and readied himself to be admonished. Through the wire, he could see his great, white guru, sitting majestically on his perch. *What do I say?* he thought, but it was Charlie who spoke first. His eyes lit up, he spread his wings, and his brilliant sulphur crest rose upright on his head. 'Greetings, young man. I see you are back.'

'Hello, Charlie,' said a remorseful Max. 'Sorry I didn't say goodbye before I went away.'

'I didn't know that you went anywhere,' Charlie replied. 'I haven't had any visitors since I saw you last, and I seem to recall that you did say goodbye.'

Max was astonished. Many sunrises had come and gone since that last visit, but Charlie had spoken to no one since. *Poor Charlie, he really does have a lonely life,* thought Max.

Max told Charlie about Eden Springs, and his plan to take a flock back there. He then invited Charlie to join him, which puzzled Charlie, who thought that only Magpies were qualified to join a Magpie flock. Max disagreed. 'I'm changing the rules,' he said. 'I want people with talents in my flock, and you are the most talented person I know.'

Max offered Charlie the tour of a lifetime. It would be a chance to see the world. He would become a hero, be with friends, and would live in a place unknown to the Noisy Miners. But he doubted that Charlie would ever give up living under the protection of Humans. Freedom had always been an unrealistic dream for Charlie, for the outside world frightened him.

Charlie thought about Max's offer, for it seemed too good to be true. How Max could make it all happen was a mystery, but Charlie trusted Max and his offer had appeal. *If Max can get me out of this cage, then Max can do anything,* he thought. He doubted that Max could organise his escape, but he was happy to be proven wrong.

'Sounds good,' he said, 'but how do I get out of this cage?'

Charlie's reply was unexpected, but Max's response was immediate. 'I have a plan,' he said, hoping that Charlie would not notice that he was crossing his toes as he spoke.

Max had often fantasised about how he could help Charlie escape, but his plan was only theory.

'Your Human will be coming to feed you soon,' Max explained. 'I will swoop him just as he opens the cage door. That will be your chance to escape.'

'Sounds good,' said Charlie, and so they waited for the Human to arrive.

The Human appeared toward dusk. In one hand, he held Charlie's dinner, and with the other he opened the cage door. Max swooped, the Human ducked, and Charlie burst his way to freedom. It all happened in a flash, but then Charlie hesitated. His beloved seeds were being flung into the air.

'Hurry, Charlie,' squawked Max.

Charlie obeyed, and the two birds headed for the meeting tree where Mayzie was waiting.

Once safely perched, Charlie had a question. 'Max, do you think we could go back and get that bird seed on the ground? That was my dinner.'

Max shook his head.

Charlie looked about and began complaining he was hungry. Then he listed the things he liked to eat, but none were available in the places where Magpies normally dined. Mayzie frowned, thinking that Max had recruited a high maintenance liability to his flock. Max ignored the frown, but he too was thinking the same. Then someone appeared who could solve their problem. The good Human had come out of his house, and Max recalled how this nice man would feed his feathered visitors.

The trio landed on the good Human's lawn and were soon enjoying its owner's hospitality. The Magpies were given mince, and Charlie was given crackers.

'Hello, Cocky. Pretty Cocky. Cocky want a cracker?' said the good Human.

Charlie loved the attention, but Mayzie was not sure that she wanted someone in the flock who stole the limelight. She felt a touch of envy.

Once eating was over, Max took Charlie home to meet the family. He explained Charlie's fear of Noisy Miners, and that he had special dietary requirements. Grandma was not impressed.

'He looks big enough to look after himself,' she grumbled.

'The Noisy Miners gang up and peck me,' Charlie pleaded.

'You need to toughen up, kid,' Grandma scoffed.

Max sprang to Charlie's defence. 'Cockatoos don't have the fighting skills of Magpies, but they have other talents that Magpies do not.'

'What good are his talents if we have to spend all day looking after him?' Muriel protested.

'Don't worry, Mum, it's only for a day or two. Charlie and I are going back to Eden Springs.'

There was a brief silence, for that was the first time Max had told his mother he was not staying long. He braced himself, for he knew he was in trouble.

'You didn't tell me that,' Muriel squawked.

'I have come back to gather a flock to keep Alice company,' Max explained.

'And who have you got in your flock?' asked Muriel.

'Just Mayzie and Charlie at this stage.'

Muriel frowned. 'That doesn't sound like much of a flock, and Charlie isn't even a Magpie.'

Charlie flapped his wings in indignation. 'Max has appointed me an Honorary Magpie.'

'There is no such thing as an Honorary Magpie.'

'Quality mother,' said Max. 'I am only recruiting quality.'

Muriel changed her tone. 'I will talk to Horatio then. I am sure that he will want to go with you.'

'Who's Horatio?' Max asked.

'Horatio is Alice's secret admirer,' said Muriel. 'Apparently, he has done nothing but mope ever since she left.'

Max chuckled. 'You mean the scrawny kid from the neighbouring kingdom. I doubt that he could make the distance to Eden Springs.'

'You've been gone a while, Max. Horatio has grown a bit since then.'

Max continued his chuckle. 'You can talk to him, Mum. I need to find a Pigeon.'

Muriel waved her wings in exasperation. 'He wants to build a flock,' she said. 'So far, he has his girlfriend and a Cockatoo, doesn't want Horatio, but now he wants a Pigeon.

'

5

PIGEONS

Finding a Pigeon seemed a simple task to the youthful Max who never anticipated anything ever going wrong. He began his Pigeon project the next morning, but soon discovered that he had a lot to learn about Pigeons.

Max had met a Pigeon at the Wilderness Windmill. His name was Homer, and he was a champion racer. Homer had told Max that if he ever wanted to know how to get to a place, all he had to do was ask a Pigeon. Max wanted a better way of getting to Eden Springs, and so he headed to the shops where the Pigeons hung out. He landed close to a small group standing around a rubbish bin. 'Do any of you guys know how to get to Eden Springs?' he asked.

The Pigeons looked at each other and then at Max. 'How would we know?' said one. 'We never leave these shops.'

'But Pigeons are world travellers. They know where everything is,' Max replied.

The Pigeons looked puzzled, but then the plumpest of them said, 'Oh, you need to speak to a homing Pigeon. We don't do that travelling thing.'

'Are there homing Pigeons around here?' Max asked.

'Oh yes, we see them all the time,' said the plump Pigeon. He pointed toward several fast-moving dots in the sky. 'Look, there are some flying over now.'

'How do I get to speak to them up there?' Max asked.

'You have to catch them at home of course.'

'But where do they live?' said Max as he watched the dots disappear into the distance.

The plump Pigeon pointed to the road next to the shops. 'Follow that road because that is what the Pigeons do,' he said. 'It probably goes past their home.'

'So, if I follow the road, I will find them.'

'Probably.'

The direction was simple; just follow the road. It sounded easy to someone who had not long before found his sister in the wilderness.

Max followed the road, but the Pigeon had not told him how far. The road went forever. Cars whizzed in both directions and buildings flanked both sides, while poles offered the only resting places for a wandering Magpie. There were no shady trees or places to eat and drink.

Eventually, Max came upon a vacant block of land in which was a puddle of water and some tall grass. A fellow Magpie was stalking insects at the edge of the grass. Max landed on the ground and greeted the Magpie. 'Do you happen to know if any homing Pigeons live around here?' he asked.

The Magpie looked up. 'Just keep going until you come to the big, fat cow. The Pigeons live near there, but what business would a Magpie have with a Pigeon?'

Max explained that he was planning to lead a flock to Eden Springs, but first he had to get directions from a Pigeon. 'Would you like to join my flock?' he said.

The Magpie seemed interested and asked, 'Where is Eden Springs?'

Max pointed to the hills. 'See that range of hills in the distance.'

'That far!' said the Magpie.

Max shook his head. 'No, we have to cross over those hills.'

'Eden Springs is on the other side of those hills,' the Magpie exclaimed.

'No, that is where the Mallee Plain begins.'

'What is the Mallee Plain?'

'The Mallee plain is a dry wilderness where only the toughest bushes survive,' said Max.

'Where is Eden Springs then?'

'In the middle of the Mallee Plain.'

The Magpie gave Max an odd look and shook his head. 'I thank you kindly for your invitation, but I think I will stay where I am.' An awkward silence followed, and then he spoke again. 'Oh look, a grasshopper.' Then he disappeared into the tall grass.

Max waited for the Magpie to return, hoping that he would change his mind, but the Magpie never came back. *Perhaps I should work on my sales pitch,* thought Max as he resumed his journey.

He flew on, but he had doubts about the Magpie's directions. The road was travelled by countless motor vehicles, which made it an unlikely place to find a cow. He was just about to put the Magpie on his *Untrustworthy Magpie* list when a cow came into view. A statue of a cow was standing on the roof of the Fat Cow Restaurant.

Max landed on the cow's head. From there, he could see a Pigeon loft behind the restaurant. He flew down to the loft's open doorway, which surprised all those inside.

A large Pigeon stepped out. 'I think you might be lost, mate.'

'No, I'm not lost, I'm looking for directions,' Max replied.

'You aren't lost, but you're looking for directions.'

'That's right.'

The Pigeon turned to the other Pigeons. 'He sounds pretty lost to me, fellers. What do you think?'

They all cooed in agreement.

'I'm not lost,' Max insisted. 'I just don't know how to get to where I want to go.'

The Pigeon put his wings on his hips. 'Look, us homing Pigeons are sick of all you other birds taking the mickey out of us. Magpies don't need directions because they never go anywhere. Now buzz off.'

The Pigeon went back into the loft, leaving Max standing at the door. He did not know what to do. Homer had said that if he wanted to know how to get anywhere, he should ask a Pigeon. But Homer had failed to mention that Pigeons were an unfriendly lot who did not like helping people.

'Homer said I should ask a Pigeon,' Max stammered in desperation.

The Pigeon stopped and turned. 'Homer, did you say Homer?'

Max frowned. 'Yes, Homer, the champion. I met him at the Wilderness Windmill.'

'You met the famous Wing Commander Homer at the Wilderness Windmill?' The Pigeon was repeating what Max had just said, but the Pigeon's tone was one of disbelief.

'Sure did,' said Max, 'but we are on first name terms. I call him Homer and he calls me Max.'

The Pigeon beckoned Max with his wing. 'Come in and tell us your story. We would like to meet someone who is on first name terms with the famous Homer. These are my friends, and I am Trailblazer, but none of us know anyone famous.'

Max followed Trailblazer and discovered that Pigeon lofts have a distinctive odour. 'I take it you guys don't use an outside toilet?' he asked.

Trailblazer laughed. 'We have all the latest home comforts in here, including an inside toilet.' He pointed to the floor.

'What a great idea,' said Max, wanting to appear polite, then he quickly changed the subject. 'I'm about to return to Eden Springs, but I want to go a different way.'

'What do you mean, "return to Eden Springs"?' queried Trailblazer. 'Magpies don't fly that far.'

'Magpies can do anything they want,' Max replied, indignantly.

Trailblazer had his doubts. 'I would like to see you make that journey. In fact, I'm finding your whole story very hard to believe.'

'I can prove it,' Max snorted.

'How?'

'If you come with me to Eden Springs, that will prove it.'

A lady Pigeon had been listening, and she was about to save Max's day. Her name was Penelope, and she had many suitors in the Pigeon loft, including Trailblazer. However, she had yet to make a choice, for she was waiting for one of them to impress her. 'I think you are being very rude, Trailblazer,' she said. 'You should help the nice Magpie. I like nice people.'

Penelope's words brought a change in Trailblazer's attitude. He looked at Max. 'Okay, I will help you. We can leave for Eden Springs now if you like.' Then he glanced toward Penelope, hoping to see approval.

Max was stuck for words, but Penelope was not. 'See you when you get back, Trailblazer,' she said. 'This is your chance to live up to that odd name your parents gave you.'

Max had his guide and Trailblazer had found a way to impress the beautiful Penelope. They left the Pigeon loft and arrived at Gum Tree Park late that afternoon, where Max was questioned by his mother. 'How many Magpies did you recruit for your flock today?' she asked.

'No Magpies, but I'm leaving in the morning and Trailblazer is coming with us.'

Trailblazer bowed graciously toward Muriel.

'Hello,' she said, and then she turned to Max. 'Let me see if I have this right. You leave tomorrow morning and all you have in your flock is your girlfriend, a Cockatoo, and now a Pigeon.'

'It's a start,' said Max.

Muriel shook her head.

6

THE GIRLS UNITE

Max's flock gathered early the next morning, and Max called the roll.

'Mayzie.'

'Present.'

'Trailblazer.'

'Ready to go, Captain.'

'Charlie.' There was silence. 'Charlie!' There was more silence.

'WAKE UP CHARLIE!'

Charlie blinked his eyes. 'Did somebody say my name?'

'Just say present, Charlie,' whispered Mayzie. 'Max is calling the roll.'

Charlie winked. 'I wasn't really asleep,' he chuckled.

Max had never been in charge of a flock before, but he thought that a roll call would be a good way to start. However, the sideways whispers were giving him second thoughts.

Muriel, Grandma, and Aunty Jenny were there as well, adding an air of excitement to the occasion.

'You can't leave yet,' said Muriel. 'You have to wait for Horatio. He told me that he wants to go with you.'

Max rolled his eyes. 'Well, the scrawny kid had better hurry, for Eden Springs awaits.'

No sooner had Max spoken before another Magpie joined them. The newcomer was powerfully built and quite handsome. Mayzie introduced him. 'Max, meet my cousin, Horatio. Good looks run in the family, don't you think?'

Max gasped. The once scrawny kid had turned into a Magpie he-man.

'Pleased to meet you,' said Max, as he thought, *I have a feeling that Alice is going to be even more pleased than me.*

'Glad to join your flock,' said Horatio. He spoke in a deep, impressive voice that Max found intimidating. Max hoped that Horatio was not the type to throw his muscle around, because he had a lot of muscle to throw, and Max needed to stay in command of a tight ship. He turned to his family. 'Sadly, it is time for us to say goodbye.'

'Who are you saying goodbye to?' Grandma asked.

'You, Mum, and Aunty Jenny.'

'But we're coming too,' said Grandma. 'We can't rely on you to recruit Magpies, and Alice needs girls for company.'

Max stood in shock as the others all laughed. It appeared that Grandma had successfully convinced the whole family to join Max's expedition.

'You didn't see that one coming did you, Max?' Mayzie giggled.

'You knew?'

'Haven't you learnt by now that us girls know more than you think?' Mayzie giggled some more.

At that moment, Dopey arrived. 'I am going to miss you guys, and Nebbie said to say goodbye.' Having said that, he took a deep breath and continued. 'As Master of Ceremonies for this auspicious occasion, it is my formal duty to speak on behalf of all those gathered here today to wish Max's band farewell.'

'But you are the only one gathered here to bid us farewell,' said Max. 'The rest of us are going.'

'I know,' said Dopey, 'but I didn't know that when I wrote my speech.'

'Let's go,' said Grandma. 'We haven't got time to listen to any more speeches.'

The flock took to the air and headed for the hills, leaving a solitary Dove in charge of Gum Tree Park. Dopey waved them goodbye.

7

ON THE ROAD AGAIN

The flock maintained a leisurely pace because Grandma's best flying days were behind her. Max wanted to reach the Church of Nowhere in three days, provided Grandma could keep going. Once there, he planned for the flock to rest for a day before going on.

Everyone was in high spirits as they left that morning because the gorge was only one sleep away. Max had told them of its splendour, and all wanted to see it for themselves. They followed the creek to the foothills, where they rested for the night. Next morning, they entered the gorge.

The gorge amazed them all, for Max had not exaggerated its splendour, but it amazed Trailblazer the most. He had flown over it many times, but never had he seen the shimmering waterfall or listened to the gurgling water. He had never heard the frogs or smelt the ferns. Flying fast and high was how you won a race. He had been to so many places, but on that day, he realised that he had seen none of them.

Everyone enjoyed the day as they slowly flew from one end of the gorge to the other. They camped that night at its far end, from where Max hoped to reach the Church of Nowhere by the following night. This next part of the journey had previously taken Max two days, for he had to follow a twisting road, but now he had a navigator. Trailblazer could take them cross country in half the time.

To Max's delight, his Pigeon recruit did not let him down and they arrived at the church the next afternoon. On arrival, Max announced that the flock could rest there for a day because Charlie and he had important business elsewhere. Everyone wanted to know where they were going, but Charlie told Max not to tell. He believed that a good leader should always be a little mysterious.

Charlie had become Max's mentor on matters of leadership, for Max's father had told Max that he did not have leadership ability. This worried Max who now had Horatio to consider, because everyone thought that Horatio would make an excellent leader.

'You should tell us where you are going,' said Horatio.

Max shrugged. 'Everyone will find out when the time is right,' he said.

Charlie nodded approvingly.

Next day, Charlie followed Max along the route Max had once travelled with a Kangaroo called Skippy. They flew across fields and fences, and finally down into a wooded valley. Their destination was the Well-meaning Wildlife Park, and once there, they headed straight to Brian's cage.

As always, the Humans had left the cage door open. 'Come out, come out, wherever you are,' Max squawked.

Brian peeped through the open door and saw that his brother had returned. With a voice of smug satisfaction, he said, 'Oh, you are still alive I see; change your mind about finding Alice? You have finally decided to come back here and live with me.'

'No, it is you who is coming to live with me,' said Max.

'Never. It is a dangerous world out there. Living in a cage is much safer.'

'RUBBISH!' screeched Charlie, who had been listening.

Brian noticed Charlie for the first time. 'Is he with you?' he scoffed.

Max nodded. 'Meet my friend, Charlie. He has spent most of his life in a cage. I've brought him along to convince you that freedom is better than captivity.'

'He should still be in a cage,' Brian sniggered.

Charlie became indignant. 'I once liked living in a cage like you, but Max has made me realise that the Humans who keep us in cages are not our friends. I now have real friends, and real friends look after each other.'

Charlie's words caused Max to think back to the day he first met his great, white guru. He saw Charlie as his teacher, but he never realised that in some ways, he was teaching Charlie things at the same time. Charlie never knew what it was to have a friend until Max showed him the meaning of friendship.

But Brian remained unmoved. His only thought was for his safety, not finding friends. He wanted Max to stay with him, so that he could boss his younger brother as he had always done. It was then that Max noticed another Magpie in a cage some distance away.

'Who is in the other cage?' Max asked.

Brian shrugged. 'Some crazy prisoner they brought in. He just sulks all day and has yet to utter a single word.'

Max wondered if he could recruit the locked-up Magpie, but asking a crazy person to join his flock was probably not a good idea. However, it would do no harm to wander over and talk to him.

The sullen Magpie realised someone was coming and turned his back. He was in no mood for visitors. Max stood in front of the cage and made a polite greeting. Unexpectedly, the Magpie spun around, because the Magpie recognised Max's voice, and Max recognised the crazy person's broken beak.

'Dad, what are you doing in jail?'

The crazy Magpie stared at his son but said nothing.

Charlie's brain went into overdrive, for Max had just called the crazy person, Dad. *Just how many members of Max's family are in jail,* Charlie wondered. *Could it be that Max belonged to a family of Magpie criminals?*

'Don't worry, Dad,' said Max, 'I have Charlie with me. He will undo the catch on the door and get you out of there.'

Charlie hesitated, but then shrugged. If Max was a criminal, then he was about to become one too. He juggled the latch and the cage door swung open.

The prisoner was out in a flash, and he slapped Charlie on the back. 'Well done, my son. Max has told me about your talents, but I never believed him until now. Call me Albert.'

These were the first words Albert had spoken since his capture.

Charlie's chest swelled with pride. Albert had just called him *my son.* He had been officially welcomed into Max's family, and he did not care if that made him a criminal. But Max felt hurt. Never in his whole life had his father ever given him such praise. Max had told Charlie that his father was a bad person, but Charlie was seeing someone nice.

The three went back to Brian's cage, but Brian had retreated into the corner. 'Come out, Brian. We have to leave,' Max pleaded.

'I told you, it is a dangerous world out there. I'm staying right here.'

Then Albert spoke. 'Get out of that cage you stupid boy, before I come in there and rip your wings off.'

The unexpected sound of his father's voice shocked Brian into action. He leapt out of hiding, saw his dad, and hopped out of the cage. 'H-hello, Dad,' he stammered.

Max's hurt feelings turned to amusement, for Charlie was seeing Albert's brutal side and Albert was seeing Brian's true colours. 'Follow me,' squawked Max, and to his delight, they did as he said. In that moment, he felt that he could become a leader.

Unfortunately, Max's moment of self-confidence was short lived, for once away from the wildlife park, he began to worry. *What have I done?* he thought. He already had concerns that Horatio might undermine his command, but now he had his dad to worry about as well. Added to this, Alice had fled home to avoid being killed by their dad, and he was about to bring them back together. He was going to betray his sister, but what choice did he have? He could not let his dad rot in jail.

They arrived back at the church and an amazing family reunion followed, but Max wondered just how long the joy would last.

8

MORE RECRUITS

Max had another task to perform before leaving the church, and that was to free Lofty. Again, Charlie's talents would be needed to get the job done. Next morning, the two of them approached the graveyard but stopped when they heard voices. They hid behind the graveyard gate and listened.

'Good morning, Bruce,' said Lofty.

'Good morning, Lofty, and my name is Garry, not Bruce.'

'Not much ever changes in their lives,' Max whispered.

Charlie nodded. 'I know the feeling.'

Max looked at the catch on the gate and asked Charlie if he could unlatch it.

'Easy. Watch this.' Charlie perched on top of the gate, then reached down and grasped the catch in his beak. The catch gave a click and the gate swung open. Meanwhile, Lofty and Garry continued their conversation.

'Garry, my name is Garry, I tell you the same thing every morning.'

Max flew over and landed beside them.

'Look, Lofty,' said Garry. 'The city boy is back, but you wouldn't remember the city boy.' Then he chuckled, for he liked teasing Lofty about his poor memory.

'Hello, Max,' said Lofty. 'I forgot to ask you last time. Did you find your sister, Alice?'

Garry frowned. 'How come you can never remember my name, but you can remember everything about the city boy?'

'I always remember my nice visitors,' said Lofty. 'Now tell us, Max, did you find Alice?'

'Sure did,' said Max, 'and do you remember me asking you about her Emu friend?'

'No point in asking Lofty about other people's friends,' Garry scowled. 'He can't even remember his own.'

'Her name is Giselle,' Max continued.

'That is a ridiculous name for an Emu,' Garry interrupted. 'There would not be an Emu in Australia with a name like that.'

'I'm not asking you. I'm asking Lofty,' Max snapped.

Max had hoped that Lofty would instantly recognise the name, but apparently not. He just stood there, puzzled. Then he spoke.

'How come you know my mum's name?' He had forgotten the conversation he had with Max a few days before, but Max was not surprised.

Max told them about his plan to reunite Lofty with his mother. Charlie had already opened the gate, and everything was in readiness for Lofty to escape. He would become the newest member of Max's flock.

Garry's face turned glum. 'Lofty, you can't go. You're safe here, but the trip could be dangerous.'

'Sorry, Garry, but I have to go.'

For the first time ever, Lofty called him Garry, which did not escape Garry's notice. *Has he been kidding me all this time*, Garry wondered, but that was a minor issue to what was troubling him now. 'You can't go, Lofty. You are my only friend. Who am I going to talk to once you are gone?' There was desperation in Garry's voice.

'You have all your Sheep friends,' Lofty suggested.

'They don't speak to me. They call me a grump. You're the only person who speaks to me.'

Max listened to Garry's soulful plea and then had an idea. 'If we can find a hole in the fence, you can come with us, but you may not like where we are going.'

'Why?'

'Where Lofty comes from, the Sheep call each other Bruce.'

'I don't care. I like Lofty calling me Bruce, but I can't go because there are no holes in the fence.' Garry sounded stressed.

'How do you know?' Charlie asked.

'Because I've already looked you stupid bird.'

'No harm in checking again,' said Charlie. He set off to inspect the fence that divided the graveyard from Garry's paddock. A short time later, he returned with bad news. 'Garry is right, there are no holes in the fence.'

'I told you,' Garry scoffed, and then he looked at Lofty. 'Well, that's it then. Goodbye my old friend. I'm going to miss you, but you should go with Max and be with your family.'

There was a short silence as they all reflected on the sadness of the occasion, and then Charlie spoke once more. 'You could always get through the gate I found.'

'What gate?' Garry exclaimed.

'There is a gate at the far end of the fence. I just opened it in case anyone knew of a Sheep that wanted to wander through.'

Garry was gone, and moments later, he was back, bounding over tombstones in a dance of celebration.

'I guess you are part of my flock now,' Max laughed.

'Lead on,' said Garry. 'I'm with you guys.'

As they wandered back to join the others, Max asked Charlie, 'Why did it take you so long to tell us about the gate?'

Charlie chuckled. 'He needed to be taught a lesson for calling me a stupid bird.'

9

THE ROAD RUNNERS

From humble beginnings, Max's flock had grown to seven Magpies, a Cockatoo, a Pigeon, an Emu, and a Sheep. He gathered his flock around, for it was time to explain the next part of the journey. Suddenly, Lofty yelled, 'Ouch!'

A boy was standing near the corner of the church, and he was holding a slingshot. Lofty had just been shot in the butt. Apparently, the boy often passed by the church and was always shooting Lofty in the butt. Garry had seen it happen many times, but he could do nothing to help his friend. This time, however, Garry was not stuck behind a fence. The boy was about to get everything he deserved.

Garry dropped his head and charged. The boy took flight and ran into the graveyard, slamming the gate behind him. Garry stopped at the fence and glared at the boy, while Lofty enjoyed the irony. Lofty's Human tormentor was trapped in what had been Lofty's prison.

Albert made ready to swoop the boy but then noticed the slingshot. The moment that destroyed his life, flashed before him. It was the same flashback that always haunted him, but this time he understood it. The last thing he recalled seeing before his beak had been smashed, was a slingshot in a boy's hand. But he could never explain his injury. The pain, the disfigurement, and the eating disability it caused, changed his life forever. That was when he began to hate the world, and when people began to hate him. If only he had known that a slingshot was a weapon that fired a stone, he might have been able to make people understand.

Albert pointed to the slingshot. 'A boy was holding one of those when my beak got smashed,' he said. 'The only thing I remembered after that was waking up under a pile of leaves.'

'You must have been a victim of Slingshot Sam,' Max remarked.

Albert looked at Max in bewilderment. 'Who is Slingshot Sam?'

32

Max told the story of Slingshot Sam, which was a story Dopey had once told Alice. Slingshot Sam would go on a rampage in Gum Tree Park, shooting Doves with his slingshot. His reign of terror only ended when his parents confiscated the weapon.

'You should have told us how you broke your beak,' said Max. 'We could have told you about Slingshot Sam. He must have mistaken you for a Dove and tried to hide your body under leaves.'

Hearing Max tell the story was a revelation to Albert. His children had the answer to the thing that had traumatised him. If only he had talked more about his beak, his life could have been so different.

'I stopped talking about my beak long before you were born, because no one believed me,' Albert explained. 'Life becomes hard when people don't understand how you feel.'

'Well, you can expect an easier life from now on,' said a reassuring Max. 'Your flock now understands what you have been through.'

The group looked at the frightened boy cowering in the graveyard and then reflected on the evils of Human behaviour. Everyone had a bad story to tell, after which, Albert saw no point in swooping the boy. A single act of revenge was never going to change how Humans behaved.

The boy remained trapped in the graveyard while Max continued his morning briefing. He announced that Trailblazer would be their guide for the rest of the journey, for he could show them a way not blocked by fences. Max hated fences because they stopped Mother Nature's creatures from roaming across her lands. Birds could fly, but creatures like Garry and Lofty had a problem.

'Today, we follow the highway to avoid running into fences,' announced Trailblazer.

'But what if there are fences on the highway?' asked Muriel.

'Humans never put fences that stop them going places,' explained Trailblazer. 'They leave the highway as a fence free zone.'

Everybody was ready to leave, but then a problem emerged.

'You will have to go without me,' said Grandma. 'My aching wings will take me no further.'

Everyone stopped and looked at a soulful Grandma, painfully moving her wings up and down. They could not leave without her, but they did not know how to fix her aching wings. Garry had the answer. 'Hop on my back,' he said. 'Max can vouch that I give excellent rides.'

Max had once ridden on Garry's back, and this horseplay had given Garry the idea. Grandma accepted the invitation, and everyone cheered. They were ready to go.

Max's flock now had both flyers and a ground crew, plus a grandma with a foot in both camps. However, her involvement with the non-flyers soon attracted attention. The Humans who whizzed by in their cars were surprised to see an Emu running beside the road and a Sheep lumbering behind. But Grandma was the icing on the cake. She was riding the Sheep like a Jockey, with an assortment of birds cheering her along. Pictures began appearing on Facebook, and Max's flock soon had a name. Humans going past in their cars were shouting, 'Go you Road Runners, go.'

For two days, the fame of the Road Runners grew. People began waiting for them by the side of the road, and they would give them food and drink as they went by. The generosity of the Humans puzzled Max who still wrestled with the question, a*re Humans good or bad people?'*

10

LEADERSHIP

Max doubted that he could ever be a true leader. He was an accidental leader that people turned to because he knew what had to be done, but a day would come when he would have nothing further to offer. A new type of leader would then take charge. The new leader might be Horatio, who charmed everyone with his charisma and good looks, or it might be his dad, who relished the power that came with leadership.

His dad had said that Brian was a born leader, and Max grew up believing leaders had to shout and frighten people. He could never do that. But Max took for granted the trust that people put in him, for he did not see trustworthiness as a useful quality for leadership. Fortunately, Charlie knew different. Unknown to Max, Charlie had enlisted Trailblazer's help to build Max's confidence.

Trailblazer had just completed a forward reconnaissance flight and had returned to report his findings. 'Commander Max, I have just met a Magpie and he wants to join our troop,' he said, 'but when I told him you were our leader, he lost interest.'

'How does he even know me?' Max asked, 'and why are you calling me Commander?'

Trailblazer shrugged. 'Pigeons always call their leaders Commander, and I have no idea how the Magpie knows about you. Perhaps you are more famous than you think.' He winked at Charlie who had come to hear the report.

'I'm not famous, and I'm not really a leader,' said Max. 'I'm just doing what has to be done.'

'Don't overthink things,' said Charlie. 'You are our leader. Just keep doing what you are doing. People will soon tell you if they are not happy.'

Max asked Trailblazer to take him to the mystery Magpie.

'Certainly, Commander,' said Trailblazer, and the two took off together. They landed a short distance from the mystery bird and could see him huddled on a branch.

'Do you know him?' Trailblazer asked.

'I don't think so,' said Max, 'but he looks a lonely individual. I will go over and have a chat.'

Max joined the mystery Magpie who remained staring at the ground. 'Good afternoon,' he said.

The mystery Magpie did not look up. 'G'day,' he mumbled.

The Magpie's voice sounded familiar, but Max could not place him. 'I heard you might like to join my gang,' Max said.

'You wouldn't want me. My people don't want me. They cast me into the wilderness.'

Max looked closer at the downtrodden stranger.

'Bernard?'

The Magpie looked like Bernard, sounded like Bernard, but he did not speak like Bernard.

Bernard nodded. 'I guessed it was you when the Pigeon said that you had a sister called Alice.'

'But what happened to your grand way of talking?' Max asked.

'Oh that. I only used that to impress the idiots who made me their leader.'

'But why are you no longer their leader?'

Bernard looked up. 'You and your sister blew my cover.'

'How did we blow your cover?' Max asked. 'We never knew you had a cover.'

Max thought back to how Alice had met Bernard. At the time, Bernard was the Grand Master of the Kingdom of Bernard, and he spoke in a sanctimonious manner. Max recalled how Bernard was upset because Alice had visited the Great Gandor and not been eaten. He declared her to be an evil witch and had cast her into the wilderness. When Max visited Bernard sometime later, he was given the same treatment.

Bernard looked into the distance and explained what had happened. He told that when a boy, his parents had adopted a young Eagle. The Eagle was sick from bushfire smoke and appeared to have been orphaned. Bernard and the Eagle grew up together, and when old enough, they left home to look for the Eagle's parents, but in vain. All they found was the fire-damaged tree where the Eagle once lived, which the Eagle reclaimed as his home.

As time went by, the Eagle became known as the Great Gandor, and all small creatures lived in fear of him. They called his tree the Lookout.

Meanwhile, Bernard had tried to join the nearby Magpie kingdom but was rejected, so he asked his Eagle friend for help. Bernard told the Magpies that the Eagle was the devil, but he had the power to keep them safe provided they made him their Grand Master.

Bernard gave a low chuckle. 'Can you believe the suckers swallowed the scam? It was only when you and Alice visited the Great Gandor and survived, that the Magpies realised I had no special powers. The game was over, and they threw me out.'

'Sorry about that,' said Max.

'It's all in the past,' said Bernard. 'I was never cut out to be a leader anyway, and I am so glad that I don't have to talk that fancy way anymore, but I do miss the delicious worms that came with the job.'

Things are seldom as they first appear, Max mused to himself, but he could relate to Bernard's problem. 'I don't think I'm cut out to be a leader either,' he said.

Trailblazer heard Max's words and decided to join him. 'Bernard, tell our commander that you have heard that he is a great leader.'

Bernard obliged. 'The Pigeon tells the truth, Commander Max. I have heard it said that you are a great leader.' However, he did not let on that it was Trailblazer who had said it.

Max was cautious of Bernard's compliment, because Bernard was by far the greatest conman he had ever met. But he was impressed by Bernard's loyalty to the Great Gandor, and loyalty was a quality Max considered important. He invited Bernard to join his flock, and a surprised Bernard gratefully accepted.

11

THE SURPRISE

The Magpies were first to be awake the next morning, and they performed their dawn chorus with great gusto. The non-Magpies shook themselves from their slumbers and glared at their companions. It was time for breakfast, but they did not have to forage, for an assortment of food lay nearby, a gift from the Humans. There were seeds, fruit, sheep pellets, and a tub of water.

The Road Runners feasted and then set out for the day. Trailblazer scouted ahead, but he had a quick word with Max before leaving. 'I have a surprise for you today,' he said.

'Tell me what it is,' said Max.

Trailblazer Laughed. 'Patience, Max. You will find out in good time.'

Max wondered what the surprise could be, for there had been so many surprises since leaving home. His family joining the flock had been a surprise. Rescuing his dad had been a surprise, and being called Commander had been a surprise, although Brian and his dad refused to call him by that title.

Max would have preferred everyone to call him Max, even though Charlie told him that being called Commander was a compliment. Charlie said the troop called him Commander to show their support, but the sullen attitude of the males in Max's family had him worried. He told Mayzie that he intended to abdicate the leadership once they reached Eden Springs, but Mayzie's reply had been, 'Max, let's talk about that when we get there.'

Max was the commander of the flock, but on the home front, Mayzie was the boss. Reconciling his domestic life with his working life was not easy. At times, he had found himself thinking back to those carefree days, like when he met B2 scratching under a bush. Max wondered if his Black Bird friend was still a carefree spirit, or if growing up had grounded him as well.

One thing did please Max, however. Bernard and his dad had formed an instant friendship. He had never known his dad to have a friend, but the two former Grand Masters appeared to have much in common.

There was so much for Max to think about as they travelled the highway that day, but he had no way of knowing that Trailblazer was about to add to his list of things to ponder. It happened when Trailblazer shouted, 'Surprise.' They had come to the end of the hills, beyond which lay the Mallee Plain.

Everyone was amazed by the vast expanse that lay before them, but Max was disappointed. He had hoped that Trailblazer's surprise was something more exciting, for Max was well acquainted with the view that the plain offered.

'Is this your big surprise?' Max muttered.

Trailblazer ignored the negative response. 'Behold, what do you see, Max?'

Max did not reply.

'Max, what do you see?' Trailblazer repeated.

Max looked once more at the plain. 'I see red dirt and scrub. What else is there to see?'

Trailblazer laughed. 'Can you not see that distant row of trees?'

Max looked again. The trees were so distant that they were almost out of view. He nodded.

'Do you know what those trees are?'

Max shook his head.

Trailblazer spread his wings. 'Behold, for yonder lays the Great River. Those trees grow upon its bank.'

Max went numb, for the Great River had been the thing that had changed their lives. Alice had always dreamt of finding the river, and it was this dream that had caused them both to be so far from home. But Alice had given up on her dream, and Max saw the irony. He had no ambition to find the river, but there it was, snaking its way along the distant horizon. He had been the first to see it, albeit, only in the distance. He stared at the trees, and then wondered if one day, he might help Alice realise her dream.

12

<h1 style="text-align:center">LAW AND ORDER</h1>

The flock followed the highway down to the plain. By now, most of the Humans who travelled the highway had heard about the Road Runners. They would slow their vehicles as they went by, and many stopped to take photos. Some threw scraps of food, and everyone wondered where the Road Runners were headed, but the Road Runner show was about to end.

That evening, Trailblazer announced that there was no longer a need to follow the highway, for the Mallee Plain had no fences.

'Wonderful,' said Garry, but Trailblazer continued. 'Unfortunately, it could be tough for the ground crew because they will have to push through scrub.'

'That sounds horrible,' said Garry, but Lofty saw no problem.

'Don't worry,' he said. 'You're going to love it, Garry. There is nothing more satisfying than having scrub drag on your feathers. It takes all the itches away.'

'But I don't have feathers,' growled Garry.

Lofty looked at his friend, his head tilted to one side. 'You're right,' he said. 'I hadn't noticed that before.'

Garry shook his head and walked away.

The following day was one of joy for Lofty, for crashing through bushes brought back memories of his boyhood, but Garry was not happy. It was apparent to all, that Sheep were not designed for going through scrub. Lofty had never seen him so grumpy. Time after time, he would have to untangle his woolly friend from a bush. The flock would gather around, and everyone would hear Garry curse. The language shocked some, but Grandma just laughed. 'It's alright for you lot,' she would say. 'You just fly away, but I have to sit here and listen to him complain.'

Garry's difficulties were slowing progress, which gave Trailblazer a problem. The waterhole where he hoped to stay that night, was

42

becoming out of reach, but the only other option was the Crows' Windmill.

The Crows who guarded that windmill and kept all the water to themselves, were on a very short list Max called his *Vermin I Despise* list. He had a score to settle with those Crows.

'We will go to the Crows' Windmill,' said Max, but Trailblazer was not sure. He explained that Pigeons never went there. If they did, they got the same treatment as other birds. Being denied water at the windmill had made crossing the plain the most dangerous part of a Pigeon race.

'It's time we put the Crows in their place,' said Max, 'and I have a secret weapon.'

Max explained his plan, and later that day, he approached the windmill. The rest stayed some distance behind. That way, they could sneak up and hide while Max kept the Crows distracted.

As expected, the Crows flanked Max when they saw him coming. They attacked him, pecking at his feathers. It was the same tactic Max had experienced before, and as before, he took refuge in the same bush. The bush stood in a clearing that was soon filled with his enemies.

The Crows' leader stepped forward and looked at Max, his eyes glaring. 'I know you,' he said. 'Still thirsty I am guessing, so you have come back to sit in your bush again.'

Max remembered the leader's evil caw, but he ignored the unfriendly tone. 'Can I have a drink of water please?' he asked.

'No. Now get going and die of thirst like you should have done last time.'

'But you have enough water for everyone. If you are nice to your guests, people will like you.'

The leader shrugged. 'Perhaps you are right. It is rude of us to ask you to leave. Please feel free to stay in that bush. It will make your body easier to find in a day or two.'

Max inwardly smiled as he listened to the Crows' sniggers, and none saw the Road Runners sneaking up behind them. 'You would not be so mean if I had a flock with me,' squawked Max. He stepped out of the bush.

Evil Crow laughter filled the air, and the leader shouted, 'You are the only Magpie stupid enough to be in these parts. Leave now and die of thirst or stay and we will kill you where you stand.'

'Time to welcome more visitors,' Max squawked.

Nothing happened.

'TIME TO WELCOME MORE VISITORS!' Max's screech was much louder this time.

Suddenly, the Crows heard Magpie squawks, and moments later, a flock of Magpies landed in front of them.

'Where have you all been?' growled Max. 'You were supposed to come the first time I called.'

'Sorry, Max,' said Horatio. 'Trailblazer was telling us a great story, and we wanted to hear how it ended.'

There was a bizarre moment as everyone waited for Max to reply, but he had nothing to say. Maintaining discipline was one of the reasons that he did not want to be a leader. Fortunately, Trailblazer and Charlie were next to arrive, ending Max's awkward impasse and further confusing the Crows.

The Crows had no idea what was happening, but the leader stood his ground. 'We will fight you to the last Crow,' he cawed. He looked around to his fellows, but they were gone. The idea of being the last Crow had no appeal.

Then Lofty crashed the scene. 'Sorry I'm late, everybody. The bushes kept getting in my way. Not all birds can fly you know.'

The leader looked at Lofty, not realising that a greater problem was coming from another direction. Garry was charging from the other side of the clearing. He was covered in twigs and leaves, a legacy of trying to keep up with Lofty. The leader heard him coming. He turned. A warrior, adorned with vegetation, an apparent camouflage for battle, was bearing down on him. He went to take flight, but too late. The impact of the warrior's head sent him tumbling, and with perfect timing, Lofty stomped his foot, pinning the leader to the ground.

'Just hold him there,' said Max, delighted to see his plan in action. His secret weapon, the ground crew, had the Crow leader right where he wanted.

The leader lay pinned, shocked by his sudden change in circumstance. It appeared that death was upon him, and his life flashed before his eyes. Some of what he saw, he regretted, particularly the part where he told Max to die of thirst, for Max's beak was in his face.

'My flock is here to bring law and order to this land,' Max squawked. 'In future, you will allow all creatures to drink at this windmill, particularly the Pigeons. They will keep us informed of any bad behaviour, and we will return if necessary. You will also treat Magpies with respect. Do you agree to my terms of surrender?

'I agree,' said the leader, his voice quivering.

'Release the captive,' said Max.

'Certainly, Commander,' Lofty responded. He lifted his foot and stood to attention, but then Garry stepped in. He pushed his snout into the leader's belly, keeping him pinned to the ground. Garry was feeling grumpy and needed someone to abuse.

'Stand down, Garry,' Max ordered.

Garry snorted, and the leader became one of the few to ever discover how unpleasant it is to have a Sheep snort in your face.

'Stand down!' Max repeated.

Garry stepped back, feeling pleased, for the snort had given him some satisfaction.

The leader staggered to his feet. 'Can I go now?' he pleaded.'

Trailblazer strolled over, his chest stuck out like a conquering general. He looked the leader in the eye. 'You can expect regular visits from Pigeons from now on, and you will be nice to us.'

'We will,' whimpered the leader.

Max waved his wing. 'You may go,' he said, and the leader flew off to join his defeated militia.

'Thank you, Max,' said a grateful Trailblazer. 'When I get back, I will see that you are awarded *The Order of Honorary Pigeon*, the highest award that a non-Pigeon can receive. You have done a service to all and put me in great favour with the beautiful Penelope. She will see me as a hero when she hears that I have won an agreement for Pigeons to drink here.

Max felt honoured. Being a leader came with rewards. Mayzie might not have to worry about him abdicating after all.

13

THE FICKLE POWER OF COMMAND

The Road Runners camped by the windmill that night. The ground crew chose a spot by the water trough while the flyers found comfortable bushes.

It was just before bedtime when the Crows came to drink at the trough. The day had been warm, and the Crows were thirsty, but Garry still felt grumpy. 'Beat it,' he growled. 'You once refused our commander to drink here, so you can all go thirsty for the night.'

Lofty interrupted. 'Who's our commander?'

'Max.'

'Who's Max?'

'Our commander.'

'You will have to introduce him to me,' said Lofty.

'Okay,' said Garry, who was used to his friend being vague by bedtime because his memory would already be asleep.

The Crows' leader took advantage of the distraction. He jumped onto the trough, but a drowsy Lofty saw what happened. 'Hello, Mr Crow,' he yawned.

Lofty's friendly greeting had foiled any chance of a quick drink.

'Get off or I will push you in,' Garry shouted.

The leader retreated to the protection of his companions who were standing close together, which was not a good idea. Garry saw his chance. He could smash their tight formation with one, well-directed charge. He lowered his head and snorted like a bull, but then Max arrived. Max had heard the shouting and come to investigate. 'What is the problem here?' he asked.

'The Sheep won't let us drink from our trough,' complained the leader.

Max frowned. 'Please don't call it *your trough*. This water belongs to everyone, and my friend was just giving you a little scare to remind you of that.'

Garry took a step toward the Crows and glared. 'Out of my way, Max. I'm about to do more than scare them. I'm about to murder a murder of Crows.'

Max spread his wings. 'As your commander, I order you to stop.'

'But, Commander, they wanted you to die of thirst.'

'I know,' said Max, 'but we must not copy their bad behaviour. Our job is to teach them a better way.'

'We will be nice from now on,' the Crow leader pleaded. The other Crows nodded in agreement.

'You can't believe them,' said Garry.

'We have to set the right example,' said Max.

'But, Commander—'

'STAND DOWN, GARRY! Let the Crows drink.'

Garry skulked away and lay on the ground beside Lofty. He shut his eyes, not wanting to watch. Meanwhile, Lofty was already asleep, dreaming that he was still running through scrub.

As Max went to leave, an evening breeze began to blow, waking the windmill from slumber. Its blades began to turn, and Max assumed that it was calling him. Its groan was inviting him to roost there, an invitation he could not refuse.

Max had developed a strange liking for windmills, having stayed with one on his first journey. Somehow, a windmill's pump could always lull him to sleep. He decided to roost on the windmill and Mayzie joined him, but she had no such fond memory of windmills. She stayed a short while, but the noise kept her awake. Finally, she could stand it no longer. 'I'm off to sleep elsewhere,' she squawked. 'I don't understand how you can sleep on this noisy thing. Sometimes I think you are a bit strange.'

'Okay,' said Max. 'See you in the morning.'

Those who witnessed the parting of the honeymooners each had their own thoughts on the matter.

Oh dear, thought Charlie.

Good for you, thought Albert.

I'm going to give Max a good talking to, thought Grandma.

Meanwhile, Max was thinking, *This is probably the last chance I will ever get to sleep on a windmill. Surely, she can see nothing strange in that.*

Mayzie joined Muriel who was surprised to see her arrive. 'You and Max have a quarrel?' she asked.

'Max would rather sleep with a windmill than me,' Mayzie sobbed.

'Muriel laughed. 'Don't worry, Max is a typical male, and all men act strange at times, but I know he loves you more than a windmill.'

'I hope so,' Mayzie mumbled, and then she closed her eyes and was soon asleep.

But back at the windmill, Max was listening to the rhythm of its pump, but it was not putting him to sleep. Mayzie had abandoned him there. It seemed that the power of command had been drained from his body.

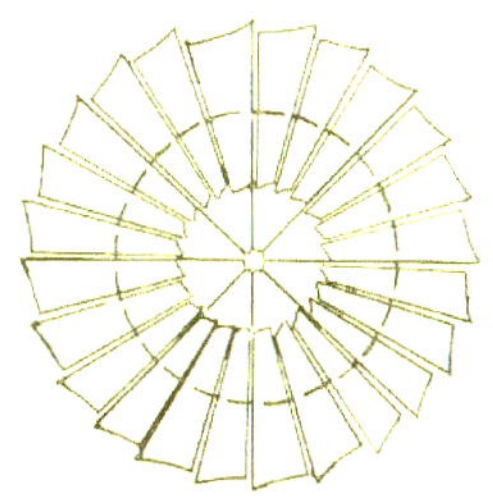

14

MIRACLES DO HAPPEN

Next morning, Garry asked Lofty, 'Do you still want me to introduce you to our commander?'

Lofty frowned. 'Sometimes I worry about you, Garry. You ask the strangest things. Why would I want to be introduced to Max when I have known him forever?'

Garry smiled. His friend's memory was awake.

Spirits were high that morning, for Trailblazer had told everyone that they would reach Eden Springs by nightfall. But it did not take long for Garry to begin growling every time a bush pulled on his wool. Grandma would tell him to stop complaining, but then a branch would whack her off his back. It was then her turn to complain, which made Garry laugh. Having a jockey cheered him up.

It was late in the day, and Alice was sitting on the water trough, talking to Horsie. A Pigeon landed alongside her.

'Good afternoon, Alice,' said the Pigeon.

'Good afternoon, Mr Pigeon,' said Alice. 'How is your race going?'

Alice was not surprised that the Pigeon knew her name, for homing Pigeons sometimes visited Horsie's trough. It was not on their normal flight path, but on hot days, a detour to drink there had prevented many a racing disaster.

'My name is Trailblazer, and I am on a quest, not in a race,' said Trailblazer.

'And how is your quest going?' asked Alice.

Trailblazer spread his wings in triumph. 'Today, I complete my quest; a task set by the beautiful Penelope. When I return, I shall seek her hand in marriage.'

'I didn't realise that Pigeons were such romantics,' Alice replied. 'I think you should talk to the Magpie boys about romance, but what exactly is your quest?'

'I am the scout for the Road Runners,' said Trailblazer. 'They will be arriving shortly with their commander.'

'Who is their commander?'

'Max,' was the reply.

'I have a brother called Max,' quipped Alice, 'but I don't know any commanders by that name. Who are the Road Runners?'

Trailblazer spread his wings once more. 'The Road Runners are the most famous flock in all the land, and your brother is their commander.'

Horsie looked at Alice. 'Shall I push the delusional Pigeon into the water trough?'

'No. Just let him have a drink and send him on his way,' she replied. 'I'm off to visit Giselle.' Alice had heard enough. *Quests, commanders, and famous flocks,* she thought. *Just because I'm the only Magpie in these parts is no reason for other birds to make fun of me.*

Suddenly, Alice heard the squawk of Magpies.

Horsie stepped back, startled by the flock as it landed on his trough. Alice sat aghast. She gazed at the birds perched around her. On one side was her mum, her dad, Aunty Jenny, and Grandma. On the other sat Max, Brian, Bernard, and Charlie. Horatio was sitting at the end of the trough. Alice did not know who Horatio was, but he soon caught her attention.

'How wonderful to see you all,' she gasped, and then she fixed her eyes on Horatio. 'I hope you will be staying a while.'

'We are all staying,' said Muriel. 'Max has brought us here to make Eden Springs our new home.'

'Oh yes, I meant all of you,' said Alice, realising that people were noticing how she was looking at Horatio.

'I'm staying too,' said Horatio, but Alice had tactfully turned her attention to her family.

Grandma winked at Muriel. 'It's going to be fun keeping an eye on those two,' she whispered.

'Stop it you old mischief-maker,' Muriel whispered back, and then they both chuckled.

A joyous reunion followed. Max had succeeded in his mission, but he still had one more task to complete. He left the group to look for Giselle who was close by. 'There's a surprise waiting for you at the farmyard gate,' he told her.

'Emus never get surprises,' said Giselle, but then she added, 'What is it?'

'If I told you, it would not be a surprise,' said Max.

Giselle followed Max to the appointed place where everyone had gathered. 'Where have all these Magpies come from?' she asked.

'My family have come to live with me,' said Alice.

'Oh, what a wonderful surprise,' said Giselle. 'I'm so happy for you, Alice.'

'That is not the surprise,' said Max.

It was time for Charlie to introduce himself. 'Hello, Giselle, my name is Charlie, and I have come to live here too.'

'Hello, Charlie,' said Giselle. 'What a pleasant surprise. It will be nice to have a Cockatoo living here. You will be great entertainment for Colin.'

'That is also not the surprise,' said Max. He pointed to a bush. 'Please meet Garry.'

Garry wandered out from behind the bush. 'Hello, Giselle.'

'Hello, Bruce,' said Giselle, and then she turned to Max. 'Where is Garry?'

'You just said hello to me,' Garry snorted.

'But Sheep are called Bruce,' said Giselle.

'WHAT!' roared Garry. 'Don't tell me that stupid Emu is finally going to get his way. I am never going to change my name to Bruce.'

'Did you just call me a stupid Emu,' growled Giselle.

'No. I was talking about *that* stupid Emu.' He pointed to Lofty who was peering over a bush.'

'You have a shocking memory, Garry,' shouted Lofty. 'You were told that all the Sheep around here are called Bruce.'

Max's surprise was not going to plan, but that mattered little to Giselle.

'LOFTY!' she shouted.

'SURPRISE!' shouted the others.

There was Magpie carolling, Sheep bleating, Cockatoo screeching, and Emus dancing. Colin could hear the fuss from the house, and he asked his mum to push him down to the gate. The party continued with Colin in the middle, a broad smile on his face.

Trailblazer was surrounded by celebration, but he did not feel part of it. The excitement of the reunion made him homesick. *I should be getting back to the loft,* he thought. He had succeeded in his quest to help Max. That alone should win him the hand of the beautiful Penelope, but he had done more. He had forged a treaty with the evil Crows, allowing Pigeons to drink at their windmill. He was about to go down in Pigeon history, and Penelope would have to be impressed.

Grandma gave Max a look of approval. 'I told you, Max, nothing stays the same for ever. Even people change. You have made your dad a much nicer person, and you have brought happiness to all those around you.'

Max had once thought that only a miracle could undo all the bad things that had happened in his family, but somehow, he had made that miracle happen.

15

YOU CAN'T PLEASE EVERYONE

Max had felt a sense of pride when Grandma praised him, but then she added the words, 'Oh, by the way.'

'What?' asked Max.

Grandma frowned. 'Last night's behaviour must never happen again.'

'What did I do wrong last night?'

Grandma gave Max her sternest look. 'A husband must always protect his wife at night, but you wandered off and slept on a silly windmill.'

Silly windmill! thought Max. It appeared that Grandma had no appreciation of how great windmills were. He would have to explain their virtues to her, but then he realised there would be no point. Grandma always knew best.

Alice invited everyone back to her place that night, which was in the tree above Horsie's stable. The Magpies accepted the offer, but Horsie declared the tree as having a two Magpie limit. He had seen the mess the Chooks left under their perches and did not want the same happening on his roof.

The flock headed for another tree, leaving Alice where she was. Mayzie perched next to Max with the other Magpies perched around them. Bernard began to snore.

'That's it, Max,' said Mayzie. 'It's time we had our own tree, and I want the one over there.' She pointed to a tree near the gate.

'What about the tree by the Chook house?' asked Max.

'Why?'

'It's a bit closer.'

'Max, closer is not better. Besides, that one is nearer to where I saw some Crows hanging out. I don't like that Neighbourhood.'

'Is that your only reason?' Max asked.

'No,' said Mayzie. 'Grandma agrees with me. She said the tree I want shows that I have excellent taste.'

Max was the commander of the Road Runners, and about to become the Grand Master of a kingdom, but when it came to choosing his home, Mayzie had the last word and she had Grandma's backing.

The newlyweds slipped away and took up residence in Mayzie's chosen tree, but then Max began to worry about Alice. Everyone had left her alone in her tree. He had failed in his duty as a brother, and Alice would be upset with him. But Mayzie could tell what Max was thinking. 'Stop looking over at Alice's tree,' she said. 'Alice has Horsie for company.'

That was the night Max discovered that it was impossible to keep everyone happy, particularly the girls in his family. For the first time, he thought he understood why his dad had spent so much time in his man tree. But Grandma was right. His first duty had to be for Mayzie. Grandma's lecture had done its job.

Eventually, both Magpies were asleep, but then Mayzie woke up. She peeped across to Alice's tree and began to giggle. 'Check out your sister,' she said, nudging Max in the ribs.

Max blinked his eyes and looked to where Mayzie was pointing. He could see Alice in the moonlight and beside her was Horatio. 'You don't have to worry about Alice,' said Mayzie, 'It looks like Horatio has volunteered to take that responsibility off you.'

Max was relieved, and he too had a chuckle.

'I thought a budding detective like you would have guessed that was going to happen,' said Mayzie.

'I'm not sure that I want to be a detective anymore,' Max replied.

'Got something else in mind?'

'A clown.'

'A clown!' exclaimed Mayzie. 'Why would you want to be a clown?'

'Grandma said that I like to make people happy, and she is right.'

'But clowns make people laugh,' said Mayzie. 'Could you do that?'

'You're laughing at me right now,' said Max.

'But could you be a leader of our flock if you were a clown?'

Poor Max. It had been a busy day and he needed sleep, but Mayzie had woken him up and wanted to talk, and her questions were becoming difficult. 'I will always be our leader because you want me to,' Max yawned, 'but someone will have to take my place if I am not here.'

Max had been waiting for the right moment to tell her that he might be going away, but somehow, he had just let it slip.

'WHAT!' squawked Mayzie. 'Where would you be going and what could be more important than staying here and leading our flock?'

A startled Max replied, 'There is something I have to do.'

Mayzie stared at Max but said nothing. Her silence told him that he was in trouble. He looked toward a distant tree where a solitary patch of white was just visible in the moonlight. 'I may have to leave again,' he said, looking at the lonely shape. 'Charlie has asked for my help to find him a girlfriend.'

16

THE RESTLESS WANDERER

And they all lived happily ever after, seems a likely ending to a story about the outcast Magpies who had found a new home at Eden Springs. The family were together again, and everyone seemed happy. Max had been appointed the Grand Master of the Kingdom of Max, although he insisted that everyone still call the place Eden Springs. Fortunately, Albert was not upset by Max's appointment, despite having once been the Grand Master himself. Albert was friendless when he was the Grand Master, but he now had Bernard as a friend. Bernard was also a former Grand Master, and he too had been friendless in the role. The two former Grand Masters had a lot in common.

But it was Max's sister who was the happiest of all. She had been swept off her feet by her Prince Charming. Horatio was the most handsome Magpie she had ever met, and she was already dreaming of the family they would be starting the following year. But Mayzie was less optimistic about her own prospects of starting a family because Max would not settle.

Max was restless. He was still the adventure-seeking detective looking for a challenge, but Eden Springs had no challenges to offer. He was a Grand Master but was not comfortable with the title. He thought it had come to him by accident. He was not the strongest, the best looking, the most skilled, or the best fighter. As a boy, Alice had giggled and called him *Adventure Boy,* while his dad had told him that he was not leadership material.

Max had become the leader of a famous flock that the Humans called the Road Runners. He had made better lives for his family and friends, but he still felt a failure. He had promised Charlie a better life at Eden Springs, but Charlie was not happy. Charlie wanted to find a girlfriend, but Max had brought him to a place where there were no Cockatoos. He felt obligated to help his friend, but he had no idea where to find a normal Cockatoo, let alone one who would put up with Charlie's eccentric behaviour.

17

THE WEDDING

Back in the city, another bird was enjoying fame. Trailblazer had negotiated a treaty with the evil Crows and Pigeons could now drink at their windmill. This deed of great valour had seen him reap the ultimate reward, the hand in marriage of the beautiful Penelope. No other suitor could match his feat, and all had withdrawn from the contest.

Penelope chose her wedding day with great care, for everything had to be perfect. She chose a Saturday night. Saturday was the day that the Pigeon owner cleaned out the loft, a task made necessary because the Pigeons all used the inside toilet. Dusk was also when the owner replenished the feeding trays and water bowls.

Penelope wanted a traditional, Pigeon wedding, and when all was in readiness, the ceremony began. The couple exchanged a wink and a nod, followed by a hip-hip-hooray from all in attendance. What followed was an outburst of feasting, flapping, and food fights, otherwise known as a wedding reception. Seed was scattered from one end of the loft to the other, and when the owner looked in the next morning, he thought to himself, why did I bother cleaning in there yesterday?

It is strange how marriage changes a person, and in the weeks that followed, people began to notice that Trailblazer had lost his competitive edge. He had been an up-and-coming star, always among the first to arrive back at the loft, which is how Pigeon races are judged. Most blamed married life for his loss of form, but the true culprit was Max. Max had taught Trailblazer the folly of always being in a hurry, for there was more to life than just winning a race.

Trailblazer had crossed the land many times, but never at the slow pace and low altitude of a Magpie. In Human terms, Trailblazer had begun to smell the roses. Often, he had flown over the gorge, but Max had taken him through it. Trailblazer was now detouring through the gorge whenever he got the chance, but this was costing him a place on the podium.

Strangely, Pigeon owners do not know that Pigeons have a podium ceremony at the end of a race because Pigeons all abide by the golden rule. *What happens in the Pigeon loft, stays in the Pigeon loft.*

18

A VISIT FROM TRAILBLAZER

Trailblazer wanted Max to know that he had married the beautiful Penelope, but news travels slow in the Magpie world. Unlike Pigeons, whose job description includes the carrying of messages for Humans, Magpies are a stay-at-home lot who know little of outside happenings. If Trailblazer wanted his good news to reach Eden Springs, he would have to deliver it himself.

He landed on Horsie's trough, and its owner was quick to see him arrive. Horsie kept a close eye on his trough, for his trough and his stable were his two most favoured possessions. He did own other things, such as a cart, but he held little affection for that.

'Hi Horsie,' said Trailblazer. 'Do you know where Max is?'

Horsie looked toward the veranda where the Magpies were gathered around Colin's wheelchair. Evelyn had just brought out treats, and Colin was handing them out. Colin loved the game of deciding which Magpie he would favour next. He knew nothing of a pecking order but that did not matter, for Max had banned that tradition anyway.

'Hey Max, your Pigeon friend is here,' Horsie neighed.

The flock were quick to gather on Horsie's trough, leaving Colin bemused by their sudden exit. Evelyn heard the flap of the take off and came out to investigate. 'What did you put in their treats?' Colin stammered. 'They've all gone to get a drink.'

Evelyn had noticed that Colin had begun to put a greater effort into speaking, and she was putting it down to his friendship with the Magpies. She looked across to Horsie's trough. 'I think they're talking to that Pigeon,' she said.

Horsie was also looking at the gathering of birds, for it was causing him concern. 'If you guys want a drink, then have one,' he said, 'but if you just want to talk, please do it somewhere else.'

Horsie was a creature who worried about what he drank. Some called him a health-nut. He was happy to let others drink the water at his trough, but he cringed whenever a bird bathed in it. Sometimes, birds did even worse, which was why he seldom let the trough out of his sight.

Fortunately, Max knew how Horsie worried about the quality of his water and suggested a gum tree where they could talk. A short time later, Colin heard loud carolling and could see what was happening in the tree. The flock were singing, *For He's a Jolly Good Fellow* and were slapping Trailblazer on the back. Usually, Magpies performed such celebrations away from Human eyes, but they trusted Colin never to tell what he knew about secret Magpie business.

Max told Trailblazer about Charlie's problem and asked if he could help find Charlie a girlfriend.

'I will have to let you know,' he said.

'Why can't you tell me now?' Max asked.

'I will have to ask my wife first,' said Trailblazer, thinking his answer would have been obvious to Max, but apparently not.

'Do husbands normally ask their wives for permission to do things?' Max asked.

'Pigeons do,' said Trailblazer. 'When everyone lives together in the one loft, it's the only way we get to survive. What did Mayzie say when you asked her if you could help Charlie?'

'We haven't actually discussed any details yet,' said Max. He turned to Mayzie. 'You're happy for me to help Charlie, aren't you?'

'No.'

'No what?'

'No, I'm not happy.'

'Why?'

'Because you haven't ever asked me properly.'

Trailblazer laughed. 'Oh Max, you get yourself into so much trouble.'

'He sure does,' said Grandma. 'Max is a slow learner when it comes to the feelings of others.'

'How come?' Max protested. 'I aways try to do what is right for everyone.'

'I know,' said Grandma, 'but it will be for nothing if you forget their feelings along the way.'

'Sorry, Mayzie,' said Max. 'I don't want to hurt your feelings, but Charlie's feelings are hurting too. I don't know what to do.'

Mayzie glanced at Charlie, whose worried look told how much her answer meant to him. 'If Trailblazer can go, then you can go as well,' she said.

Everyone gave a sigh of relief, but then Mayzie added a few conditions. 'You will take no risks. You will eat proper food. You will stay out of the rain. You will get enough sleep, and you will not talk to strangers.'

Max took it all in, but he doubted that he could oblige with the last request because he talked to everyone. But four out of five he could manage. 'Okay,' he said.

The matter appeared settled, but then Mayzie added, 'I would like one more thing.'

'What?'

'Bring me back a present.'

Grandma rolled her eyes. Max's father had not been a good role model. He needed coaching, for he did not understand the basic rules of harmonious, married life. 'It looks like I will have to give him another talking to,' Grandma muttered to herself.

19

SMELLING THE ROSES

Trailblazer headed back to the city, but he did not go straight home. He spent the night in the gorge, for he shared Max's liking for the place. He arrived home the next morning and was in big trouble. Penelope had been awake all night, worrying where he was. Added to this, the Pigeon owner was annoyed. Trailblazer was no longer performing well as a racer and going AWOL had made matters worse. But one bird's trouble can be another bird's delight. Trailblazer's bachelor rivals were enjoying Trailblazer's dilemma and had begun calling him, Pigeon Pie.

'You will finish up as pigeon pie if you don't improve your racing performances,' Penelope warned, and then she frowned at the other birds for suggesting such a thing.

How fickle people are, thought Trailblazer. *You are a hero one day and a has-been the next.*

Penelope asked Trailblazer if he was late because he had been injured.

'No,' he said.

'That's bad luck,' cooed one of the bachelors. 'The last bloke who came in late had the decency to die from Falcon wounds the next day.'

A little Pigeon peeped out from a nesting box. 'Are you going to die, Trailblazer?'

Penelope had heard enough. She pushed Trailblazer out the door. 'Come on, we're out of here,' she said.

Penelope took Trailblazer to the privacy of a rooftop, although a rooftop is normally not the place where people seek privacy. There they perched, in full view of the bachelors who were doing their best to beak-read.

Penelope stared at her husband and asked the question that everyone was asking. 'Why have you lost interest in winning races?'

'That is something I cannot explain,' said Trailblazer, as he looked toward the hills.

'What then?' said Penelope. Her wings were on her hips.

A cheer came from the watchers in the loft. Wings on hips meant that Penelope was laying down the law.

'Come with me and I will show you,' Trailblazer replied. He took off and Penelope followed.

A second cheer came from the loft. 'Run, Trailblazer, run.'

Trailblazer kept flying until he reached the gorge, where he landed in a tree close to the waterfall. Penelope landed beside him. 'What is this place?' she asked.

'Smell the air, listen to the water, and look at all that is around you,' said Trailblazer.

'Nice,' said Penelope.

'It is better than nice,' said Trailblazer, 'and it is something Pigeons know nothing about because Pigeons only know about racing.'

'But racing is what we do because it is what all our friends do,' said Penelope. 'You can't give up racing and live in this tree all your life.' She was being practical, but she understood how Trailblazer felt. The place was beautiful.

'This is only half the story,' said Trailblazer. 'Those people back in the loft are not our friends. Come with me and I will show you what real friends look like.'

20

FRIENDS

The Pigeons flew hard and arrived at Eden Springs later that same day. They landed on Horsie's trough, which caused its owner some concern. Stories of city roofs covered with pigeon poo worried him. Yesterday, there had been one Pigeon on his trough. Today, there were two. If the trend continued, tomorrow there would be four, and the next day, eight. Horsie stopped thinking at eight because he did not know what number came next.

'Max isn't here,' he said.

Trailblazer was surprised by Horsie's abrupt manner but did his best to ignore it. 'Hello, Horsie,' he replied. 'Do you know where I can find Max? I have brought my wife to meet him.'

'Try the cabbage patch,' snorted Horsie. He flicked his mane, the sweep of horsehair almost knocking Penelope into the water.

The Pigeons made a hasty retreat and Penelope was not impressed. 'I think that Horse was trying to get rid of us,' she said. 'You told me the people here were friendly, but I'm not so sure.'

'Don't worry about him,' said Trailblazer. 'Horsie gets edgy when a strange bird lands on his trough, but he will be alright once he gets to know you.'

They found the Magpies foraging in the cabbage patch, but everyone stopped when the Pigeons arrived. Penelope was suddenly the centre of attention.

'Trailblazer, you have brought your beautiful bride to see us,' squawked Mayzie.

The girl Magpies began to fuss around Penelope, asking about her wedding, her family, where she grew up, and what she liked. But no one asked if she had ever won a Pigeon race. Back in the Pigeon loft, racing was the only thing people ever talked about, and Penelope hated the subject. She was not a good racer, but the Magpies were not judging her for that. They were only interested in getting to know her better.

Meanwhile, Charlie was sitting in a nearby tree, and it took him a while to notice Trailblazer's return, but he became excited when he did. It meant that he was about to hear the verdict on his girlfriend hunt.

Cockatoos are considered intelligent, and Charlie was smarter than most, but even the smartest of birds can get it wrong when they get excited. He flew down to join the group. 'Hi, Trailblazer, did the old girl give her permission for us to go hunting for a lady? These were words out of character for Charlie and were ones he soon regretted.

There was an awkward silence as Trailblazer pointed to the gathering of girl Magpies. They parted, and there stood a frowning Penelope. All the girls were frowning. 'Meet my wife, Penelope,' said Trailblazer.

There was another awkward silence as Charlie considered his options. Disappearing down a hole in the ground was the one that most appealed, but not possible. He went into damage control, took a deep breath, and bowed. 'Absolutely charmed to meet you, my dear. You are even more beautiful than Trailblazer described, and I am so glad to see that his mother gave him permission to help me find a girlfriend.'

Penelope was relieved when she realised that only Charlie was looking for a lady, but she was puzzled by the involvement of Trailblazer's mother. However, Charlie's gentlemanly manner impressed her. 'What a charming man you are,' she said.

The awkward moment seemed to pass, but then Penelope thought some more. She frowned at Trailblazer. 'How come you told your mother but not me?'

'I forgot,' said Trailblazer, as he cast a disapproving look toward Charlie.

Max was amused, for failing to tell Mayzie was the crime Trailblazer had lectured him on the previous day. It appeared that Trailblazer had committed the same offence.

Fortunately, Charlie realised that he had gotten both husbands into trouble, but he could think of only one way to save them. He pleaded for mercy.

'You are all so lucky,' he said. 'You have each other, but I am destined to spend my life as Eden Springs' lonely bachelor.'

Charlie's pleading worked, for Penelope understood his problem. He could not leave Eden Springs without a guide. She looked into his eyes and could see how much her answer meant. Then, with true feminine logic, she decided it would be a shocking waste if such a charming Cockatoo were never to find a lady. 'Trailblazer and I are both going to help you,' she said.

There was loud applause amid which could be heard, 'I'm coming too,' and, 'so am I.' It appeared that almost everyone wanted to go, but Brian only volunteered because his father frowned at him. Horatio was also a reluctant volunteer. He only volunteered so as not to tarnish his perfect image.

Alice had a sudden thought. 'Who is going to look after Colin if we all go?'

'And someone has to stay with Grandma,' Aunty Jenny added.

'No they don't,' growled Grandma. 'I am going too, and Garry is coming with me. I once heard that Australia rides on the Sheep's back. Well, I don't know about Australia, but this old girl rides on a Sheep's back and I'm off to get my grumpy Sheep now.'

But Alice's problem gave Horatio the excuse he wanted. He could appear noble and not go at the same time. 'Alice must stay with Colin because he likes her the most,' he said, 'and I will stay with her because that is my duty.' He looked about for approval, but no one spoke.

21

THE BREAKUP

That night, Trailblazer suggested to Penelope that they roost some distance from the Magpies, but she thought it bad manners. She was enjoying the Magpies' company and saw no reason to roost elsewhere.

'When do you plan to get up tomorrow?' Trailblazer asked.

'A sleep-in would be nice,' she said. 'We have been flying all day and I am weary.'

'Then I think we should find our own tree.'

Penelope shook her head. 'I'm too tired to go anywhere, and Muriel has already invited us to stay in their tree.'

'But—'

'Trailblazer, can we please stay the night with my new friends.'

'Okay,' said Trailblazer, who was not prepared to disagree, for he was still in trouble thanks to Charlie's ill-chosen words.

The Pigeons roosted with the Magpies, but Penelope's sleep-in was cut short when a loud chorus of carolling erupted. Dawn was approaching, and the unexpected performance almost blasted her out of the tree. 'What's happening?' she yelled.

'I tried to warn you,' said Trailblazer. 'Your new friends have some odd habits you need to be aware of.'

'Can we go somewhere else?' Penelope pleaded.

Trailblazer agreed. He knew a dark corner in the hay shed, and they headed there as soon as it was light enough to see. There they stayed until late morning.

When the Pigeons finally emerged, they found the Road Runners gathered around Horsie's cart. Max had called a meeting to plan the mission, but no one knew where Cockatoos lived. Trailblazer arrived and answered their question.

'There are hundreds of Cockatoos living along the Great River,' he said. 'We can leave for there tomorrow.'

Alice's face dropped. She had always wanted to go to the Great River, but she was the one staying back. The Great River was the place where Mother Nature's creatures gathered to exchange wisdom and knowledge. It had been her girlhood dream to go there.

Aunty Jenny could see the disappointment in Alice's face. 'You go,' she said. 'I will look after Colin.'

'Not so quick,' said Horatio. 'The trip might be dangerous, and I will not have Alice facing danger. She will stay here where I can protect her.'

I always thought the pretty boy was a bit of a wuss, thought Max, but Alice was thinking things much harsher. Horatio was telling her what to do. Everyone knew how much she wanted to go to the Great River, but he was saying, 'No.'

'So, what are you telling me?' asked Alice.

Horatio put on his most impressive voice. 'I am saying that you will stay here, and as my future bride, your duty is to agree with me.'

'But I want to go,' Alice pleaded.

'I am sorry, but I cannot allow it.'

Suddenly, Alice was seeing a different side to the man who had swept her off her feet, and all thoughts of marriage vanished.

Aunty Jenny shared her anger. 'You are going,' she squawked. 'I will stay here and keep Colin entertained, and that's final.'

'Thanks Jenny, you are a wonderful aunty,' said Alice.

'It's the least an aunty can do for her favourite niece,' Jenny laughed.

Horatio changed his attitude. 'But sweetheart, we are going to be married.'

'Not a chance,' said Alice. 'I'm joining the Road Runners, and we are off to see the Great River.'

22

ON THE ROAD AGAIN

The Pigeons slept the night in the hay shed, from where the next morning's carolling was gentler to the ears. Everyone arose upon hearing it, had a quick breakfast, and assembled on Horsie's cart. Horsie discouraged birds from sitting on his trough but was happy for them to sit on his cart. Horsie hated his cart.

Max stepped forward to call the roll but then remembered the flack he got the last time he tried that. 'It looks like everybody is here,' he said. 'Let's go.'

'We're not all here,' Garry shouted.

'Who's missing?' Max asked.

'Lofty said he was coming.'

'Lofty must have slept in,' commented Penelope, who had yet to meet Lofty.

'No,' said Garry. 'That stupid Emu never sleeps in. He said he wanted to come but has forgotten as usual.'

Garry's grumpy voice carried all the way to the farmyard gate, from where Lofty's voice came drifting back. 'Hey guys, what's the hold up? I've been waiting by this gate forever.'

'I said we were meeting at the cart,' Garry shouted.

'You said the gate,' Lofty protested.

'You wouldn't remember what I said,' growled Garry.

It was time for Grandma to step in. 'Settle down, Garry. I'm about to hop on your back, and I don't want my trusty steed arguing with people.'

Penelope gave Trailblazer a worried look. 'Oh dear, people are arguing already. I don't think this is going to be a very happy trip.'

'Don't worry about those two,' chuckled Trailblazer. 'They argue all the time. It keeps the rest of us amused.'

The journey began at good pace, with Grandma holding tight to Garry's wool. But it was not long before Garry's bounding had turned to a trot. It then became a jog, and then a walk. By midday, Garry was looking for a place to lie down.

'Why are we stopping?' asked Lofty.

'I need a rest,' Garry puffed.

'Weakie,' taunted Lofty.

'It's alright for you. You're not wearing a woollen jumper, and you don't have a jockey.'

Grandma jumped to Garry's defence. She was not putting up with any arguing. 'Stop picking on my giddy-up,' she growled.

Garry was perplexed. 'What's a giddy-up?' he asked.

'A horse of course.'

Lofty rolled on the ground in fits of laughter, which was too much for Grandma. She waited for him to stop rolling and then took a firm grip on his neck. 'Your turn to be my horse,' she said. 'Giddy up.'

'Don't you ever cut your toenails?' screamed Lofty.

'You have to apologise to Garry and not call him a weakie,' squawked Grandma.

'Sorry, Garry,' said Lofty, disappointed that he was quitting an argument he was winning, but Grandma's mean tactics gave him no choice.

23

TRIPOD

It was while resting in the shade of a bush, that Garry had a random thought. 'Grandma, are Lofty and I Road Runners, or do you have to be a bird to be a member?' he asked.

'I'm a bird,' objected Lofty.

'You're not a real bird,' grumped Garry.

'Am so.'

'Prove it. Let me see you fly.'

Grandma frowned. 'Will you two idiots stop it. You are both Road Runners. In fact, you are the only true Road Runners. The rest all fly. Where do you think the name Road Runner came from?'

'I knew that,' said Lofty.

''You did not,' grumped Garry.

'Did so.'

'If you two don't stop arguing, I will squawk in your ears until your eyes water,' growled Grandma.

The threat worked. The idea of having Grandma squawk in your ears was enough to bring peace for the rest of the day.

Trailblazer estimated that it would take two days to get to the Great River, but he knew of a small waterhole where they could camp overnight. They arrived there close to dark and found the place deserted, which was a surprise. Water was scarce on the Mallee Plain, which should have made the water hole a popular gathering place, but no one else was there. They drank their fill and foraged for supper. After that, they roosted nearby, but all wondered why they were there alone.

It was just on dusk when Max noticed a smallish figure cautiously making its way to the water. The creature was half-hopping and half-hobbling. It appeared to be a small Rabbit with an injury. Max glided down and landed beside it. 'Hello, my name is Max. Are you alright?' he asked.

The Rabbit jumped in fright but then regained his composure. 'Hello, my name is Tripod,' he said. 'I used to be called Ralph, but then this happened.' Max could see that Tripod had only three and a half legs. Half of a front leg was missing.

'What have you done with the rest of your leg?' Max asked.

Tripod shrugged. 'I lost it in a bad Human's rabbit trap.'

'That sounds like such an unlucky thing to have happen,' Max exclaimed.

Tripod smiled. 'Actually, it turned out to be my lucky day.'

'That doesn't sound like a lucky day to me,' said Max.

Tripod explained. 'Bad Humans usually kill the Rabbits they catch in their traps, but I was lucky. Most of me got away.'

'But not your leg?' said Max.

'That's right,' said Tripod, holding up his stump. 'My leg was not so lucky. The trapper has it now.'

'The pain must have been horrible,' said Max.

'Yes,' said Tripod, looking down at his stump. 'It is the most painful thing you could ever imagine.'

'So how could that be your lucky day?'

'Well,' said Tripod, 'I still had a problem because Rabbits usually die after losing a leg in a trap.'

'I guess that would be a problem,' said Max. 'How come you are still alive?'

Tripod went on with his story. 'There I was, in the middle of nowhere, lying not far from the road. Suddenly, a car pulled up and I heard Humans say it had a boiling radiator. Then one of them wandered into the scrub and found me. He picked me up, put me in the car, and I was taken to a place where other Humans healed my leg. Then a few days ago, I was brought back here and set free. Being found by a good Human in the middle of nowhere could only happen on a very lucky day.'

'I still would not call it a lucky day,' said Max.

'It depends on how you see things,' said Tripod. 'For instance, today is your lucky day but you just don't know it.'

'How come?'

'Last night, a shooter was at this waterhole and so I hid. I saw him shoot every Kangaroo that came here. He's a mad man who shoots anything that moves. Some of you would have bullets in you right now if he was here tonight.'

'Why are you still here?' Max asked.

Tripod dropped his head. 'I don't know where my home is. My family lives by the ballerina tree, but I don't know how to get there.'

Max called for Trailblazer, thinking that he might know how to get to the ballerina tree, but Trailblazer was still out scouting. Penelope flew down and saw Tripod standing on his three and a half legs. 'You poor thing,' she said. 'Is there anything we can do to help you?'

'Tripod is looking for the ballerina tree,' said Max. 'I wanted to ask Trailblazer if he knew where it was.'

'Is that the big, dead gum that has two tall branches reaching skyward?' Penelope asked.

'That's it,' said Tripod, his eyes lighting up and his whiskers twitching. 'The Humans call it the ballerina tree because it looks like a Human dancing with her arms in the air.'

Penelope's face saddened, for she had bad news for Tripod. 'Trailblazer and I saw that tree this afternoon,' she said, 'but Trailblazer says that we can't go that way. That way takes us past a bad Human, and that is why he is still out scouting. He is looking for a safer way to go.'

Tripod's ears dropped. He had hoped that these strangers could help him get back to his family.

Penelope looked at Max and could tell that he was weighing up the safety of the flock against helping Tripod, but she had already made up her mind. 'What are you thinking, Max?' she said. 'We can't leave Tripod here. Sooner or later, that mad man is going to shoot him.'

These were the situations Max dreaded as a leader. He stood there, pondering, but said nothing. Finally, Penelope broke the silence. 'I'm telling Trailblazer that he has to take us to the ballerina tree,' she said.

'Okay,' said Max, but he was still not sure what to do.

24

A BAD HUMAN AHEAD

Next morning, Max addressed the Road Runners and did his best to explain Tripod's problem, but when he told them that helping Tripod required them to go through bad Human territory, some shook their head. For the first time ever, Max thought that he might be facing mutiny. At least, that was how it was until the subject of toilets came up. Brian asked Tripod, exactly where he was when he got trapped?

'I was on the toilet,' Tripod explained, 'and being trapped on the toilet is the worst thing that can ever happen to a Rabbit. After hanging on all day, you are—'

'Rabbits have toilets?' Brian interrupted. Brian wanted to know every detail about what dangers lay ahead, but he never thought that going to the toilet would be one of them.

Tripod continued. 'Yes, each Rabbit has its own special patch of ground for when nature calls, but evil trappers sometimes put their traps there.'

'That's horrible,' said Penelope.

'You had better believe it,' said Tripod. 'One moment, you are sitting in the comfort of your own privy, and the next thing, boom. Dirt flies everywhere and metal jaws come out of the ground and grab your leg. The pain is unbearable, but even worse, you are trapped, defenceless, terrified of what will happen next.'

Penelope put her wings to her ears. 'Please stop. I don't want to hear anymore. You poor Bunny.' She looked at the others. 'Don't anybody argue with Max. We have to help Tripod.'

Mayzie took Max aside and whispered, 'Penelope is right. Like it or not, we can't leave Tripod here. He has been through enough already. We have to find the ballerina tree.'

Max glared at his band of adventurers. 'We have to help Tripod,' he squawked, and he raised his wing in the air.

The Road Runners looked at Max and then at Tripod. Then they looked at each other. Suddenly, the chant, 'We must help Tripod. We must help Tripod,' echoed across the Mallee Plain.

The troop broke camp and headed for their first landmark. By now, they had a well-drilled method to navigate the plain. Trailblazer would nominate a visible landmark and the rest would aim for it. Once there, they would aim for his next landmark. In places where the scrub was thick, Trailblazer would stay close and help the ground crew steer their way through.

The first landmark for the morning was a telegraph pole, and when they reached it, they found that it stood next to a dirt road. 'From now on, we are in bad Human territory,' warned Trailblazer. 'This road will take us past the ballerina tree, but there are some terrible sights along the way. Not far from here, is a dead Fox hanging from a tree, and just beyond that are things even more grisly.'

'What?' queried Brian, his squawk sounding more like a dry cough.

'There has been a terrible crime committed against the Kangaroos. I suggest that we pay our quick respects to the victims when we get there, and then move on.'

'There are victims there?' squawked Brian, his voice almost choking him.

'Sort of,' said Trailblazer.

'Sort of?' Brian was ready to cry.

Trailblazer shrugged, 'There are bits of the victims there. I think they are the bits the Human did not want.'

'MUM!' screamed Brian, his voice strangely returning, 'you have to take me back.'

Brian knew it was pointless asking his dad or Grandma, for they would just say, 'Toughen up, Brian.'

Muriel put a comforting wing across Brian's shoulder. 'You'll be alright, son. Humans don't hurt Magpies. It is our friends we have to worry about.' She glared at Trailblazer. 'You could have told him in a nicer way.'

Trailblazer folded his wings. 'I said right from the start that I did not want to come this way, but you all voted. If you know a nicer way to tell people about the carnage ahead, let me know.'

Tripod sighed. 'Welcome to my life. You people are talking about the place where I live. It's a scary world for us Rabbits, but we are tougher than we look.'

'And we are tough too,' said Max. 'The bad Humans may hurt us, but Mother Nature's creatures will always prevail. Where is our next landmark, Trailblazer?'

Trailblazer pointed ahead. 'Just follow the road; it goes past the ballerina tree and on to the Great River.'

25

PUTTING YOUR FOOT IN IT

The road was easy going compared to the scrub, but Garry still complained about the stones hurting his feet. He decided to run on the softer ground next to the road.

'I wouldn't go there if I were you,' cautioned Tripod.

'Why not?'

'Bad Humans.'

Garry ignored Tripod's odd remark but stopped when he came to a small patch of soft ground. He noted an impressive quantity of Rabbit poo scattered there. 'Is this a Rabbit's toilet?' he asked.

'I wouldn't step there if I were you,' Tripod warned.

'Garry laughed. 'When you have spent your whole life in a paddock full of Sheep, stepping on a bit of poo is the last thing that would worry you.'

But when Garry stepped onto the Bunny toilet, he stopped laughing, for dirt flew into the air and something grabbed his foot.

'Bad Humans!' squealed Tripod.

Lofty watched his friend pulling at a trap, which was chained to a peg in the ground. Never before had he heard Garry use so many bad words.

'Oh no, this is all my fault,' wailed a remorseful Tripod.

'No, it isn't,' said Lofty. 'Bad Humans are to blame.'

By this time, Garry had pulled the peg out of the ground, but the trap was still on his foot, and it really hurt. Garry would have told everyone how much it hurt, but Tripod's lament stopped him. Tripod already knew how much the trap hurt, and little Tripod's pain would have been far greater. Garry's only choice was to man-up.

'Lofty is right, it is not your fault,' said Garry.

The Road Runners gathered around, wondering what to do. Max was in need of good advice, but his Chief Advisor was not there.

Charlie was some distance behind, examining something he had found on the road.

'Someone go and get Charlie,' Max ordered.

The Pigeons headed back while the rest stood around, and then Brian began to babble. 'I knew this would happen. We should never have come this way. I wish I was back with Aunty Jenny and Horatio. We are all going to die.'

Bernard looked at Albert. 'Are you going to tell him, or shall I?'

'I will,' said Albert. 'He is my son, after all.' Albert walked over to Brian and looked him in the eye. 'SHUT UP, BRIAN!' he squawked, and then he walked away.

'Everyone must stay calm,' said Max, knowing that the situation would test his leadership. It had been his decision to come this way, which made him responsible for what had happened. But Max was feeling far from calm. His only hope was that Charlie would know what to do.

The Road Runners sat in a circle with Garry in the middle, all staring at the contraption hanging from Garry's foot. 'We need to move away from here before the trapper comes back,' warned Tripod.

They walked some distance along the road, looking for suitable bushes in which to hide. Even Grandma walked because her trusty steed was lame. He was limping, his trap going, *clink, clank, scrape, rattle.* The noise of the trap horrified Brian. 'You have to be quiet, Garry, or the trapper will hear us,' he whispered.

Garry's head began to shake. *Oh no,* thought Lofty, *I have to stop this.* He could see that Garry was about to let fly with another colourful outburst, and so he walked over and stooped down to Brian's level. With their beaks almost touching, he said, 'Shut up, Brian.'

Brian said no more, which saved everyone from another Garry tirade, but Garry had hobbled far enough. 'That's it, I'm going no further,' he grumped. 'If that trapper comes back, Lofty can bring him down and you guys can peck his eyes out.'

Max sat with Garry by the side of the road, while the others hid in the nearby scrub. Neither talked, but Garry's mind was working overtime. Thoughts of revenge were taking some of the pain away. *Once we have him blinded, what then?* thought Garry. *Hot coals, a snake pit, a man-eating Bunyip.* These were all things he thought might be useful, but none were readily available. Then he thought of an anthill. That had possibilities. 'Has anyone seen an anthill around here?' he shouted.

Garry's fantasies ended when he saw Charlie flying toward them.

26

GOOD HUMANS

Charlie arrived, flanked by the Pigeons, and the rest of the flock gathered around.

'You took your time getting here,' said Max.

Trailblazer frowned. 'Blame Charlie. It was lucky that Penelope was with me. I couldn't drag him away from the thing he was looking at. Penelope had to give him a piece of her mind before he would come.'

Max could not imagine the beautiful Penelope being angry, but then again, he did not know her that well.

'Charlie, look what has happened,' said a soulful Garry as he held the trap in the air.

Charlie glanced at Garry and then turned to Max. 'Max, you have to come and see the fantastic object I found. It is a bit smashed up, but has red glass and metal parts, and there is wire hanging from it.'

Max ignored Charlie's excitement about a broken taillight. 'Charlie, we have a problem,' he said. 'What do we do about the thing hanging off Garry's foot?'

Garry waved the trap in front of Charlie's beak.

'Oh Garry, I hadn't noticed. You should have told me.'

Max shook his head. As usual, Charlie had been in a world of his own. 'What do we do about the trap on Garry's leg?' Max repeated.

The great, white guru thought a moment and then said, 'Ask Tripod. He knows the answer.'

'I AM NOT CUTTING MY LEG OFF!' shouted Garry.

'You don't have to,' said Charlie. 'Tripod found good Humans that healed his leg. All we have to do is find a good Human who will remove that trap.'

The guru had spoken, but everyone had doubts. It took a while for Charlie to convince them that he was an expert on Human behaviour, having studied them for most of his life.

'I will choose a good Human for you,' said the guru. 'Max and I will wait by the side of the road and Garry can hide near us. The rest of you can just fly around and be birds for a while, but don't wander far.'

'What about me?' asked Lofty.

'You can run around and be an Emu.'

'Okay, I know how to do that,' was the reply.

Max waited with Charlie, and then a car came roaring toward them. 'This might be a good Human,' said Max.

'Probably not,' said Charlie.

The car sped by, leaving them shrouded in dust. They shut their eyes and listened to the car's even louder roar as it disappeared down the road.

Then came a ute doing a more leisurely pace. 'Would this be a good Human?' Max asked.

'Don't trust utes,' said Charlie. 'The Humans who kidnapped Lofty were in a ute.'

The ute passed, but with a smaller cloud of dust.

Then came a car towing a caravan. Max watched the caravan bounce as it hit every pothole in the road, but Charlie was more interested in the car's occupants. Charlie was looking for holidaymakers, for he thought holidaymakers would be in a good mood and more likely to help someone in trouble.

'Garry, come quick and hold your trap in the air,' Charlie screeched. 'We have to stop this car.'

The car was being driven by Trevor, a recently retired police officer. Beside him was his wife, Martha. They were on their first ever, caravanning holiday, and were headed for the Great River. But Trevor had taken a wrong turn and found himself towing their brand-new van along a dirt road. Each time the van hit a bump, Martha would tell him to drive more carefully. They were not exactly in the good mood that Charlie was hoping for, but they were kind-hearted people.

Trevor lifted his eyes from the potholed road and noticed a hitchhiker ahead. As he got closer, he realised that it was a Sheep sitting on its backside. The Sheep seemed to be thumbing a ride by waving a rusty rabbit trap.

The caravanning couple were wary of hitchhikers and had made a rule never to stop for one, but this hitchhiker had them curious. They pulled over.

'Wave your trap at them,' Charlie screeched.

'Stop calling it *my trap,*' growled Garry. 'It is not my trap.'

Charlie ignored the complaint. 'Get ready to run if they are not friendly,' he screeched.

'You never told me that running could be part of the plan,' Garry bleated. 'You try running with this thing on your leg. I am probably going to finish up as lamb chops.'

'Well, no plan is perfect,' said Charlie, 'but what is the worst that could happen?'

'Lamb chops *is the worst* that could happen,' yelled Garry.

Fortunately, Charlie's gamble with Garry's life paid off. The two retirees got out of their car and Garry heard Martha say, 'Oh look, Trev, that poor Sheep. We must get that nasty trap off his leg.'

What followed was a circus.

'Martha, turn him this way.'

'I can't, he has his woolly butt in my face.'

'Martha, try to press down the spring of the trap with your foot.'

'I can't, he keeps trying to kick me.'

After much bleating and shouting, Trevor finally had Garry in a headlock. 'Keep your foot still you stupid Sheep,' he growled.

'Don't call me stupid, you silly old man,' Garry bleated, but Trevor did not understand Sheep language.

The Trevor verses Garry wrestle continued until both were almost exhausted. It ended when Martha put her foot on the trap and pressed down the spring.

'The trap is off,' she shouted. 'Wow, look at that Sheep go.'

Garry was gone, for he was in no mood to hang around and say, 'Thank you.'

27

CRASHING THE PARTY

Trevor knew from his experience in the police force, that rabbit traps had been banned for years. 'This is a problem I'm going to get the boys to fix,' he said. 'We need to catch the scoundrel setting these traps and come down on him with the full force of the law.'

Trevor was already missing his old job, but Martha did not expect to see him turn into a police officer in the middle of the Mallee Plain. 'Let's just pull over and have a cup of tea,' she said. 'You're retired now. You must learn to relax.'

Trevor parked the van a short distance along, just out of view of the passing traffic. He went to a box on the towbar and fetched two chairs and a small table. Martha went into the van and boiled the kettle, coming back a few minutes later holding a cup of tea and a tin of biscuits.

'Where's my cuppa?' Trevor asked.

'Inside, next to the stove. I can't carry everything at once.'

'A man drives all morning, and now he has to fetch his own cup of tea.'

'That's right. I'm retired too.'

'Only joking, luv.'

Meanwhile, Lofty had chased Garry into the scrub and the Pigeons had followed, for they could see them both becoming lost. All this gave Charlie a chance to go back and examine the thing he had found on the road, which left the Magpies doing nothing. The retirees soon found out what happens when Magpies have nothing to do.

Trevor was just beginning to relax in his chair when the Magpies joined the party. 'Let's use our Magpie charm to see if they will give us treats,' said Alice. She began to warble, and the rest joined in.

'Oh, how wonderful,' said Martha. 'Fancy finding such lovely birds out here. I must give them something to eat.'

'Do that and you will never get rid of them,' joked Trevor.

Martha laughed. 'Not much chance of that, Trev. Once we are gone, they will never find us. The only way we could ever finish up back here, is if you get lost again.'

'You were navigating.'

'No, I wasn't.'

'Well, I thought you were. No wonder we got lost.'

But Trevor soon had something else to fret about, for Martha had begun giving bits of his favourite biscuits to the birds. 'Don't feed them too much, luv, or you will attract more wildlife,' he warned.

'What wildlife, Trev? These Magpies are the first wild creatures we have seen all morning.'

Martha put down the biscuits and began throwing bits of stale bread instead. The Magpies scoffed the bread before the ants had a chance to realise it was raining food. Then the Pigeons arrived and joined the feast. 'Look, luv, now you're attracting Pigeons,' Trevor growled.

'I don't know where these birds keep coming from, Trev. The guidebook says nothing about Magpies and Pigeons living out here. I think I will ask for my money back when we get home.'

'Better tell the guidebook people about Cockatoos as well,' Trevor remarked. 'There's an incoming Cockatoo at six o'clock.'

'I thought I might have seen a Cockatoo when we first saw the Sheep,' said Martha.

Charlie landed a short distance from the table and announced, 'Charlie wants a cracker.'

'Good heavens,' said Martha. 'This Cocky has been educated.' She picked up the biscuit tin and threw Charlie a biscuit.

Charlie looked at Max. 'See, I can make Humans do anything I want. Watch, while I make her say, "Charlie is a pretty boy".'

Charlie repeated the words several times, and sure enough, Martha began saying, 'Charlie is a pretty boy.' The flock marvelled at Charlie's power over Humans.

Martha kept rewarding Charlie with biscuits until Trevor realised that he could see the bottom of the tin. 'Better put the biscuits away, luv,' he said. 'Heaven knows what birds you might attract if you don't.'

The words were scarcely spoken before Trevor heard a rustle in the bushes. Lofty came charging through. 'Good God, Martha, it's too late. You have just attracted a bird that could eat us out of house and home. All we need now is for that stupid Sheep to turn up.'

Baaaa.

Trevor threw his hands in the air. The bleat could mean only one thing. Sure enough, Garry came limping in behind Lofty. Trevor slumped in his chair. 'Throw a bucket of water over me, Martha. I think I'm having a bad dream.'

Martha did not reply, for she had gone to get her smartphone. She wanted a picture for Facebook, but getting the Road Runners to pose was like herding cats. Finally, she managed what would have been a perfect shot but for Charlie. He appeared to be picking his nose, but no matter, for there was no chance that he would ever see himself on Facebook or read the comments made about him.

'I need the phone now you have finished,' said Trevor. 'I want to ring my old mate, Bill. He's the sergeant in the next town.'

The Road Runners listened as Trevor made the call. Alice felt guilty for eavesdropping, but she could hear only half the conversation anyway. Trevor said 'Goodbye' and handed the phone back to Martha. 'Bill said we should wait here and see if the trapper comes back to check his trap,' he said. 'Apparently, the police have been trying to catch him for weeks. This area is a wildlife sanctuary, but the trapper comes here to trap Rabbits and shoot Roos. Bill will be here as soon as he can.'

Garry suggested that they stay and see the trapper get what he deserved.

'I second the motion,' said Tripod, who suddenly appeared from under the caravan where he had been hiding with Brian.

Then Brian appeared. 'You don't get a vote because you're not a Road Runner,' he squawked. Brian was keen to put as much distance between him and the trapper as possible, and the idea of staying could never be part of that plan.

'You are being very rude, Brian,' scolded his mother. 'I think we all should stay. Tripod and Garry deserve to see what happens to the man who hurt them.'

'But, Mum, the trapper has a gun. If we stay here, we are all going to die.'

'My turn,' said Bernard, pushing Albert to one side. He walked over to Brian and said, 'Shut up, Brian.' He spoke quietly, but his words sounded far more threatening than a shout.

Max took a vote to stay and declared the vote unanimous, for Brian was back hiding under the caravan. No one saw which way he voted.

28

A CITIZEN'S ARREST

Bill arrived in his paddy wagon, which he parked next to the caravan, making sure that everything was out of sight. He did not want to alert the trapper.

Bill was a man about Trevor's age but had a much larger belly. He told them that he was waiting for Head Office to approve his retirement, but they kept putting it off. Apparently, an officer with his keen eye for detail was too valuable for the force to let go. But everyone soon observed that Bill had lost some of that skill, for it took some time for him to notice the assortment of wildlife around him. 'What's with this lot, Trev?' he finally asked. 'You have an Emu, a Sheep, a Cockatoo, a three-legged Rabbit, and a flock of Magpies.'

Trailblazer looked at Penelope. 'What about the Pigeons? Everyone ignores the Pigeons.' He walked over and stood on Bill's foot. 'Coo,' he said.

Bill looked down. 'Oh yes, you have a Pigeon here as well.'

'I can see why he never rose to the rank of Senior Detective,' Trailblazer quipped.

'You are such a harsh critic,' laughed Penelope.

Everyone stayed by the caravan that afternoon, waiting for the trapper's vehicle to return. Many vehicles went by, but none stopped at the crime scene. Then came the sound of a trailbike, but not from the road. It was traveling through the scrub, and it stopped a short distance from where Garry had been trapped. 'Blast,' said Bill. 'He's on a trailbike.'

This was something unexpected, for the paddy wagon was not designed for chasing felons through scrub. He needed to make the arrest before the trapper got back on his bike.

Bill ran toward the fugitive and the Road Runners joined the chase, but Bill's best running days were behind him. He saw the trapper through the bushes, but the trapper saw him.

'Stop in the name of the law,' Bill gasped.

Cops still say that? smirked the trapper. 'You won't catch me,' he yelled as he ran toward his trailbike.

'I'm too old for this stuff,' Bill puffed, and he sank to his knees, but the sight of the trapper getting away made Garry's blood boil.

'Get him, Lofty,' Garry bleated.

Lofty paused. 'Why me?'

'I can't run because my foot hurts.'

Suddenly, Lofty remembered why Garry was limping. That trapper had hurt his friend, and in that moment, Lofty forgot that he was an Emu. He became Mother Nature's wrecking ball.

The avenging Emu crashed through the bushes, the noise striking fear into the heart of the trapper. The trapper turned to face whatever pursued him, which was an airborne Lofty coming over a bush. Next he knew, he was lying flat on the ground, bewildered by his rotten luck. Australia's only flying Emu had just landed on top of him.

The trapper tried to get to his feet, but Garry arrived. He butted the trapper in the stomach, sending him sprawling back to the ground. The trapper tried to get up again, but with the same result. He thought about a third try but gave up.

Bill puffed onto the scene and slapped handcuffs onto the fugitive. 'You're under arrest for trapping wildlife in a sanctuary,' he wheezed. Then he sat on the ground, gasping for breath. Once recovered, everyone made a triumphant return to the caravan. Trevor was impressed by Bill's achievement. 'He's a big bloke, Bill,' said Trevor. 'How did you manage to handle him on your own?'

Bill shook his head. 'It's all a bit bizarre, Trev, and I don't know how I'm going to explain it in my report. I don't think anyone has ever reported a Sheep and Emu making a citizen's arrest before. Head Office will probably say that I have lost the plot.'

'That's one way to fast-track your retirement,' laughed Trevor.

Meanwhile, Tripod had his own score to settle. He sunk his teeth into the trapper's ankle. 'OUCH! Can someone get rid of this crazy Rabbit,' screamed the victim of the angry Bunny.

'A Rabbit has just assaulted a prisoner in custody,' said Trevor. 'I guess that has to go in your report as well.'

'Sure does,' said Bill. 'This report will have me retired by Christmas.'

Bill pushed the trapper into the back of the paddy wagon. 'Come on,' he said. 'I'm getting you back to the station before more things happen. I don't want my report turning into something no one is going to believe.'

'It's already too late for that,' laughed Trevor.

That evening, Martha's Facebook post told how the Road Runners had made a citizen's arrest, and the post went viral. The Road Runners were becoming famous.

29

BRIAN THE BOLD

The retirees stayed where they were that night, and the Road Runners stayed with them. Martha put out a large bowl of water, but such kindness creates an obligation to return the favour. Next morning, the Magpies treated their benefactors to a rollicking rendition of their dawn chorus, staged on the caravan roof.

The light had just begun to filter through the curtains of the darkened van, and Trevor was in the twilight zone, but Martha was wide-awake. 'Don't those Magpies sound wonderful,' she said, 'and they seem so close.'

A mumble came from beneath the blankets. 'What did you say, luv?'

'I said the Magpies sound so close.'

Trevor sank his head deeper beneath the bedding because the performance was getting louder. Albert had begun as the lead warbler, but Bernard wanted a turn. He stomped over and pushed Albert aside. An annoyed Albert then pushed Bernard. The two then stomped about, pushing each other, but Grandma was not prepared to put up with such behaviour from two grown Magpies. She saw it her duty to install some discipline and began chasing the two offenders all over the caravan roof.

To those inside the van, the stomps sounded like a bombardment of bricks. Martha heard another muffled complaint come from under the blankets. 'Your crazy Magpies are about to bash the roof in. Could you please get rid of them, Martha.'

'It's morning, Trev. You need to embrace the great outdoors.'

At that moment, there was a knock at the door. 'That's it,' Trevor shouted. 'Now they're knocking to come in.'

Trevor was partly correct, for Brian was pecking at the door. He had remembered how he would stand by his cage door at the Well-Meaning Wildlife Park, and a Human would feed him each morning.

But this apparent bravery made no sense to the other Magpies because they had not been raised in Human captivity.

Martha opened the door and found Brian standing there. 'Oh, you cute little Magpie. Let me get you some bread.'

The word *cute,* in reference to Brian, was more than Alice and Max could stand.

'Teacher's pet more like it,' scowled Max.

'Scaredy-cat,' giggled Alice.

But the others only heard the word, *bread.* Martha came out with a small handful for Brian but found all the Magpies were now at her door.

'Later that morning, Trevor asked for a second slice of toast but was told that the bread was all gone. He glared out the window, searching for the culprits who had eaten half his breakfast, but they were gone as well. The Road Runners were headed for the ballerina tree.

30

SEEING A GHOST

Everyone was eager that morning. Tripod was about to be reunited with his family and the rest would reach the Great River by nightfall. Lofty was especially excited, so much so that he needed to burn off energy. He had run ahead, for he could not wait to get to where they were going.

Suddenly, Lofty stopped. Where was he? Where was he going? Why was he feeling excited? The world's most forgetful Emu was having one of his moments. He could not remember a thing.

He looked behind and saw a bounding lump surrounded by a number of smaller lumps that flew. They appeared to be following him, but as they got closer, he could see that it was Bruce being chased by birds. He guessed he was either having a weird dream or about to be caught up in a Magpie air raid. He went with the bad dream theory and laid down on the road and closed his eyes.

A short time later, he heard a familiar voice. 'What are you doing lying in the middle of the road, Lofty?'

Lofty opened his eyes. 'Hello Bruce. We're in the same dream together.'

'Lofty, you are not dreaming, and my name is Garry, not Bruce.'

'Oh,' said Lofty, looking confused.

'Don't worry, everyone,' said Max. 'Lofty has these strange moments, but they always pass.'

It was then that the retirees went by, towing their caravan. Trevor gave a loud toot on the horn and Lofty jumped in fright.

'You are so mean,' said Martha. 'That poor Emu just got the fright of his life.'

'Just getting even,' Trevor chuckled.

Lofty looked at Garry's foot. 'Are you okay, Garry, or is your foot still hurting?'

Garry smiled. The fright had restored Lofty's memory.

'Lofty is back, everyone,' Garry announced. 'A fright always does the trick. Now you know why we call him the world's most forgetful Emu.'

Lofty knew that people called him that, but he did not know why. He was just about to ask when Charlie arrived. Charlie had been lagging because he kept finding objects that required his attention, but something had frightened him. 'We are being followed,' he screeched.

'By who?' asked Max.

'By a ghost,' Charlie stammered.

Bernard whispered to Albert. 'Charlie looks very pale. He might have seen a ghost.'

'Hard to tell with Cockatoos,' said Albert. 'They only come in white.'

Max needed to know more. 'What sort of a ghost?' he asked.

Charlie glanced over his shoulder. 'It's the ghost of a Kangaroo; probably one that got shot back at the waterhole.'

These were the moments that always tested Max's leadership. He needed to keep people calm or there would be panic. 'If it's the ghost of a Roo, then it shouldn't hurt us.' he said. 'We didn't shoot the Roos.'

'So, you believe in ghosts then,' said Mayzie.

Max had never given ghosts much thought, but he realised that believing in them was probably not a good look for a leader. He decided to put the question to a vote. 'Please raise your wing or foot if you believe in ghosts.'

Only Charlie put up a wing. Several were unsure, but they would not admit to it. Max looked at Charlie. 'Better stay with the group from now on. I think the strain of the trip might be causing you to see things.'

'LOOK!' screeched Charlie, and he pointed down the road.

There, amid the distant heat haze, appeared a blurred, ghostly shape. A white apparition was bounding toward them, but then it disappeared into the bushes.

'Can we have a second vote?' said Charlie.

'Don't bother,' squawked Brian, 'I'm out of here.' He spread his wings and went to leave. The others were ready to follow.

'Wait,' said Tripod. 'I think I know the ghost. Stay here while I go back and check.'

'That's the last we will see of him,' squawked Brian. 'We are all going to die.'

'My turn,' said Alice. She walked over to Brian and in a sweet, sisterly voice, said, 'Shut up please, Brian. Tripod would not be going back if we were all going to die.'

31

AUSTRALIA'S MOST WANTED

Tripod hopped cautiously through the bushes but stopped when he thought he heard a noise. 'Is that you, Snowy?' he whispered. He raised his ears and twitched his nose.

A voice whispered back. 'Is that you, Tripod, is that you?'

'It is, Snowy. You're alive!'

A small, albino Kangaroo hopped out from behind a bush. It was Tripod's friend, Snowy. Unfortunately, albino Kangaroos are very rare, and the Humans had been trying to catch Snowy since the day he first hopped. He was on Australia's most wanted Kangaroo list and had spent his whole life on the run.

'It's good to find a friend,' said Snowy, 'but I thought you were going to stay at the waterhole until your family found you.'

'I think the Bunnies have gone to ground,' said Tripod. 'The maniac who trapped me has been shooting everything that moves. I thought he had shot all the Roos, but he must have missed you.'

Snowy shrugged. 'He's a bounty hunter, and he wants me alive. I'm worth nothing to him dead.'

'I wish I was white,' Tripod sighed.

'No, you don't,' said Snowy. 'I met a white Rabbit once. He had escaped from a Human. He said the Human was always stuffing him into a hat and then pulling him back out.'

Tripod shook his head. 'Humans are very weird.'

Snowy agreed.

Tripod beckoned Snowy to follow. 'Come with me. I have some friends you must meet.'

'Can I trust them?'

Tripod grinned. 'These guys are amazing. You don't have to worry about that bounty hunter anymore. He's behind bars because these guys captured him. I think they are the famous Road Runner gang, but I haven't asked them because gangs don't like people asking too many questions.'

Snowy nervously followed Tripod, while the Road Runners nervously waited by the roadside. Everyone was nervous.

Tripod shouted through the bushes, 'We're back.'

Brian panicked and hid behind Garry's leg, but a quick kick sent him flying. 'Oops, sorry about that,' said Garry.

'Run for your lives,' squawked Brian. 'It's the ghost.'

Albert jumped on Brian and held him down, while Grandma thought how best to quell Brian's panic. She went over and pecked Snowy on the leg. 'Nup, he feels real, definitely not a ghost,' she said.

'Have you quite finished?' Snowy asked.

'Yes, thank you,' said Grandma. 'I'm a bit disappointed though. I have always wanted to meet a real ghost.'

At your age, you will soon be one yourself, thought Bernard, but he stayed silent, for Grandma was always threatening to come back and haunt people one day.

Tripod introduced Snowy and everyone made him feel welcome. Snowy explained that he was on the run because the Humans had put a price on his head. Max suggested that he stay with the flock because Trailblazer kept them informed on the whereabouts of Humans. Snowy accepted the offer.

The group set out once more, but they did not get far before coming across Humans. The retirees had a flat tyre, and Trevor was trying to change a wheel, but he had dropped one of the wheel nuts and it had rolled under the caravan. He was lying on his stomach, but the nut was just beyond his reach.

Martha was delighted to see the Road Runners. 'Look who's here, Trev,' she said.

Trevor could just touch the nut with his fingertips. 'Hang on, luv, I've almost got it.'

It was then that Martha sighted Snowy, and her heart began to race. 'LOOK, TREVOR, LOOK!' She could not think of the word *albino*, and so she just kept shouting, 'LOOK!'

'Hang on, luv.'

'LOOK, TREV!'

'In a minute, luv. I need to get this nut.'

'TREVOR!'

Trevor staggered to his feet, hitting his head in the process, but Snowy was now hiding in the bushes.

'What, luv, I still need to get that nut,' Trevor grumbled.

'Doesn't matter now, Trev, you were too slow.'

'Women,' exclaimed Trevor, as he felt the lump on his head. Then he noticed the Road Runners. 'How come you lot are back and what are you staring at?'

Brian, whose greatest achievement as a child had been to master the art of playing with a stick, saw something interesting. He ran under the caravan and came back with the illusive nut in his beak. Then he dropped it, because it had an oily taste. The nut rolled along the ground and stopped by Trevor's foot.

'Martha, have you been training these birds?' Trevor exclaimed.

'Like I've always told you, Trev, birds are smarter than people think.'

'You're right, Martha. This bird deserves a biscuit.'

Martha shook her head. 'I can't give him a biscuit, Trev. The Cocky ate the last one this morning.'

32

A COCKATOO COURT

The Road Runners arrived at the ballerina tree, which stood a short distance from the road. The tree was strong and tall, with two massive branches reaching skyward, but not a single leaf sprouted from its grey limbs, for the tree had been dead for many years.

Tripod ran to the Rabbit burrows but saw no one. The place had been abandoned. 'The water must be gone,' he said.

'What water?' Max asked.

Tripod did not answer. He raced back to the road and disappeared into a pipe that ran under it. Max flew to the pipe's entrance. 'Are you in there, Tripod?' he squawked.

Tripod emerged just as the other Road Runners arrived. 'The water has gone,' he said.

Tripod explained that the pipe was partly blocked, and that the blockage trapped water. But the pipe had gone dry, which would have forced his family to move to their summer home.

'Where is their summer home?' Max asked.

'I don't know,' said Tripod. 'They haven't had to go there since I was born.'

Poor Tripod, thought Penelope. *He is even younger than I thought.*

Max was equally as sympathetic. 'I guess you and Snowy will have to come with us to the Great River,' he said.

The idea shocked Brian. 'They will attract bounty hunters who will shoot us,' he objected. 'We are all going to die.'

'Charlie, it's your turn to tell him,' said Bernard.

Oh no, thought Max. *Charlie is not the person to ask,* but it was too late.

Charlie took a deep breath. 'Well, as Max's Chief Advisor and authority on all things legal, I believe that telling Brian to shut up is not proper procedure. Therefore, as this matter has now been placed in my hands, and as I am the most qualified to deal with such things, I hereby call a hearing to consider Brian's grievances.'

'Why do we need a hearing?' Max growled.

'Max, you can't run a flock without rules,' Charlie explained. 'Brian has a democratic right to be heard.'

'Charlie has a good point,' said Bernard, who was always looking for a way to make mischief. 'I suggest we let Charlie proceed with his hearing.'

Max shook his head. Telling Brian to shut up had always worked in the past, but Charlie had to go and make things complicated.

Charlie stood on a rock and called the hearing to order. He asked Brian to state his complaint, but Brian had no more to say.

'It looks like I have to speak on Brian's behalf,' said Charlie, and so he continued. 'Brian has every right to object because our latest guests are not Magpies. However, there is a way out of this technical problem. I suggest that we make them Honorary Magpies.'

Everyone was confused. Charlie was supposed to be pleading on Brian's behalf, but he seemed to be helping the opposition. 'I object,' squawked Brian. 'There is no such thing as an Honorary Magpie.'

'Wrong,' said Charlie. 'Max has made me an Honorary Magpie.'

'And I'm an Honorary Magpie too,' said Garry.

'Who said you were an Honorary Magpie,' asked Lofty.

'You did.'

'I don't remember.'

'No surprises there,' laughed Garry.

Grandma frowned. 'You started this, Bernard. Now everyone is confused.'

'Brian is right,' said Bernard. 'There is no such thing as an Honorary Magpie.' Garry lowered his head and scratched the ground, causing Bernard to step back and reconsider his opinion. 'Come to think of it, Garry and Lofty do look a lot like Magpies,' he said. Trailblazer gave a sharp coo. 'And the Pigeons definitely have a Magpie look about them,' Bernard added.

Grandma gave a wry cheer. 'I'm glad that is all settled,' she said. 'I move that those not born a Magpie, shall from this day onward, be Honorary Magpies.'

'I second the motion,' said Charlie.

'You can't,' said Bernard.

'Why not?'

'Because you are the one presiding over the hearing.'

'What about me?' squawked Brian.

It was time for Max to take back control. He walked over to Brian and squawked, 'The hearing is over, so SHUT UP, BRIAN!' and then he thought, *I should have just done that in the first place.*

Max was amazed at how good it felt, telling his older brother to simply shut up. He was on a roll, and so he added a further declaration. 'From now on, Charlie will never again preside over a meeting.'

'That's a shame,' said Charlie. 'I thought I was sorting things out rather well.'

Max did not reply. 'Come on, everyone,' he squawked. 'Time is wasting. We need to get to the Great River.'

33

DESPERATION TIME

It was late in the afternoon and Max had begun to worry. The sun was hot, and everyone was thirsty, for they had been without water since breakfast. If they did not drink soon, they would not see another day.

Max thought that the scenery would change as the river got closer, but it remained the same. He needed Trailblazer to explain why this was, but he had not seen the Pigeons since leaving the ballerina tree.

'Where is that crazy Trailblazer?' growled Garry, as they rested yet again. 'I'm going to kill him if he lets us die out here.'

'How are you going to do that?' asked Lofty. 'You'll be dead.'

'We are all going to die,' squawked Brian, his throat half parched.

Max frowned. 'Stop it, Garry. You've started him off again.'

Albert strode over to Brian but did not have to speak. 'I know, Dad,' Brian mumbled, his head dropping to his chest. 'Shut up, Brian,' he said.

Bernard chuckled. 'No good telling your boy to shut up anymore, Albert. He's finally worked out how to do that for himself.'

At that moment, the Pigeons returned. 'Not long now,' announced Trailblazer.

Everyone cheered, but Max was sceptical. He had seen the Great River in the distance, and it had tall trees growing along its full length. He should be seeing the trees by now.

They continued along the road until coming to a sharp bend, and this change in direction worried Max even more. Trailblazer had said that the road would take them straight to the river, and to date, it had been without deviation. But this new course had Max thinking that Trailblazer may have sent them down the wrong road. Then, when Trailblazer said, 'I think we had better stop here,' Max convinced himself that his suspicion was correct.

'I think you Pigeons have us lost and will leave us here to perish,' snapped Max, who was no longer thinking clearly. Dehydration was taking its toll.

Trailblazer sensed Max's anxiety. 'Penelope can stay here while Alice comes with me to see proof we are not lost,' he said.

Alice was puzzled, but agreed. She followed Trailblazer, but he did not follow the road. Instead, he continued in the direction that the road had been heading. To Alice's surprise, the scrub ended at the top of a cliff that was close by. There they perched, and Alice gasped.

What lay beyond was mostly green, but not the green of the scrub. It was the green of the trees Alice had seen in the city. The scene was breathtaking but flawed. It had the mark of Human interference upon it, for everything was in straight lines and rectangles. Alice was not sure that Mother Nature would have given her approval to what was an endless landscape of orchards.

'Beautiful, isn't it,' said Trailblazer.

'Wow,' said Alice.'

'There's more.'

'More?'

'Look straight down.'

There below, pushed hard against the base of the cliff, was the Great River, and it was much wider than Alice had imagined. Soft, green willows grew along its far bank, their heavy boughs reaching out to touch the deep, cool water. Tall gums stood behind the willows, but none was tall enough to reach above the mighty cliffs on which Alice was perched.

Alice watched a family of Ducks swimming close to a thicket of reeds, and then she thought about Nebbie, the wise Koala who had told her about the Great River. He said that she would never see it because it was too far for a Magpie to fly. Alice smiled inwardly, for she was looking at it now.

34

MORE TRUST ISSUES

Alice thought about flying down to the river, but her conscience would not let her take a drink from a place that the ground crew could not reach. 'Is there a place where everyone can get a drink?' she asked.

Trailblazer explained that the cliffs ended a short distance downstream, at which point the road crossed a bridge and then went through a town. The bridge was where he was taking them.

They returned to the others and Max was eager to know what Alice had seen.

'Nothing,' she said, wishing that Max had not asked the question. Alice never told untruths, but she was concerned about Lofty. She thought that the truth might give him another burst of energy, and he would run to the edge of the cliff and fall over.

'We just have to keep following the road,' said Trailblazer.

Max had his doubts, but Alice said, 'Don't worry, Maxie, we can trust Trailblazer.'

They followed the road for a short distance before coming to another bend, but this one sloped downhill. They pushed on, their spirits almost broken, but then their spirits lifted. Around the bend was a place full of wonder. 'Is that a bridge?' asked Mayzie, but it was the endless row of tall trees that caught Max's attention. He let out a squawk of great delight. 'Alice, come with me. Let me be the first to show you the Great River.'

Max had imagined this moment since the day Trailblazer first showed him how a row of trees marked the river's path. Seeing the Great River had been Alice's girlhood dream, and Max was about to make her dream come true.

The two siblings perched on the bridge railing and looked down at the water. 'Well?' said Max.

'It's wonderful,' said Alice.

Max was disappointed. He had expected his sister to show more feeling for the moment, but he did not know that she was feeling guilt. Her thoughts were for Max's feelings, hoping that he would never discover how Trailblazer had stolen this cherished moment from him.

The rest of the flock raced under the bridge, keen to drink in its shade. Trailblazer issued a warning. 'There's a dangerous current under there. Tread carefully, or we might never see you again.'

Brian wanted to ask what a dangerous current was, but he was afraid that the answer would scare him more. He stopped in his tracks. It was gloomy under the bridge, with lots of places for a dangerous current to hide. *Best let the others go first,* he thought. Meanwhile, he would scan every dark nook and cranny, for a dangerous current could be anywhere. It might be hanging from above, waiting to drop down on him, or simply pounce on him from behind a pylon. Perhaps it was hiding in the water, making ready to pull him in.

Brian watched as everyone lined up at the water's edge, and he wondered if any would fall victim to the dangerous current. The ground crew were unlikely to die, because they were the biggest, but Penelope was the smallest. She had a good chance of meeting her doom. He waited for something bad to happen to Penelope, but she just kept drinking.

Trailblazer was first to finish, and then he noticed that Brian was standing back. 'Why aren't you drinking with the others?' he asked.

'Where is the dangerous current?' asked Brian.

'In the water,' said Trailblazer. 'Go down with the others and you should be safe.'

'*Should* be safe?' queried Brian.

'You will be perfectly safe as long as you keep your feet dry,' laughed Trailblazer.

Brian had no choice, he needed to drink, but the others were already coming back. 'Hurry up and get your drink,' said his mother. 'Everyone wants to go and find supper.'

'But I'm scared,' said Brian.

'Get down there and drink, you stupid boy,' squawked Albert.

'Dad, if I go down there, I will die.'

'Get down there NOW.'

'You're safe,' assured his mother. 'We will save you if something goes wrong.'

'But if I go down there, I will d—'

'GET DOWN THERE NOW!' squawked Albert.

Brian could imagine no harsher treatment than being denied the right to say what would probably be his dying words, but that was what was happening. He would need to keep his feet dry if he were to survive, but the riverbank appeared moist. Then he saw a ray of hope. There was a flat rock at the water's edge. He could stand on that rock and just reach the water with his beak.

Brian flew down and landed on the rock. A rock was something Brian understood. A rock was solid, it stayed put, and it never argued with you. You could always depend on a rock. But everything Brian thought he knew about rocks was about to change.

'Please don't stand on me,' said the rock.

Brian froze with fear. He looked down. A small head was looking up at him. He had never imagined that the dangerous current would be a rock with a head on it. 'The r-rock sp-spoke,' he stammered. No one bothered to answer.

'You must be a city boy,' said the rock.

'W-why?' gasped a petrified Brian.

'You have just woken me up, you are standing on me, and you have just called me a rock. Only a city boy would be that rude to a Turtle.'

Max was amused to hear someone call Brian a city boy. City boy was what people used to call him. He flew down to apologise to the Turtle. 'I'm sorry, Mr Turtle,' he said. 'You are correct. My brother does come from the city.'

'I will have you know that I am Ms Turtle, not Mr Turtle,' huffed the Turtle. 'You are as rude as your brother. You must both be city boys.'

Brian leapt off Ms Turtle as she lurched into the river. She swam away.

Max felt annoyed. He thought he had shaken off the tag of city boy, but Brian had brought him undone. His only hope was that none of the others had noticed Ms Turtle's unkind remark. Sadly, Alice was already preparing a jibe for her brothers.

'Will you two city boys stop upsetting the locals,' she squawked. 'How am I going to find wisdom and knowledge when two city boys keep upsetting everyone we meet?'

Max's annoyance went up a notch, but Brian still had a problem. He either had to drink from the river or die of thirst. He chose the drinking option, but only after Trailblazer explained in more detail, about the currents under the bridge.

Once everyone's thirst was quenched, Trailblazer suggested that they stay close to the bridge that night, for there were Humans camped not far away.

'The Humans might feed us,' said Brian.

'No,' said Max. 'Snowy has to stay hidden from Humans.'

Snowy laughed. 'Max, I'm Australia's most wanted Kangaroo. I know how to hide. You should go and check the Humans while I hide here.'

Max decided otherwise, for it was close to sunset which left no time to gamble on Human generosity. He told everyone to forage where they were. They could camp by the bridge and investigate the Humans in the morning.

35

A HERO IS BORN

Everyone had plans the next morning, but everyone's plan was different. Max suggested that they go their separate ways and meet back at the bridge late that afternoon, but Brian had already gone. Bernard said he had seen Brian sneak out shortly before the morning chorus.

'He never did like being in the choir,' laughed Max. 'I guess he will come back when he's ready.'

Brian had gone to investigate the Humans camped nearby, because Humans had always fed him in the morning. Trevor and Martha had been excellent hosts, and he hoped these Humans might be the same.

He flew to the campsite and was in luck, for the Humans were indeed like Trevor and Martha, because they *were* Trevor and Martha. Brian knocked on the door, and as before, Trevor stuck his head under the blankets.

'Could you get that, luv,' he mumbled. 'It's probably the kid next door telling us our paper is on the roof. I'm sure he throws it up there because you pay him to get it down.'

'Trevor, we are not at home. We are in the caravan.'

Trevor shook himself awake. 'Is the sun up? I need to go fishing. The fish bite best at first light. I will have breakfast later.'

Trevor rushed out the door, still in his pyjamas, and almost tripped over Brian. 'Get out of my way you stupid bird,' he growled. He grabbed a sinker from his tackle box and threw it at Brian. The sinker rolled under the caravan.

'Blast,' said Trevor. 'I needed that sinker but that stupid bird just lost it for me. Please stop feeding the birds, Martha.'

But Brian thought the sinker was a plaything, and he chased it under the van. He picked it up and ran back, dropping it by Trevor's foot. Trevor looked at Brian in disbelief.

'Martha, the Magpie that retrieved my wheel nut yesterday is here again. He must have followed us, and he just got my sinker back. He's my little hero. Do you have some mince we can give him?'

'I thought we weren't going to feed the birds, Trev.'

'This Magpie is no ordinary bird, Martha. I'm calling him Hero.' 'Stay here, Hero,' he said to Brian. 'Aunty Martha will bring you out some mince.'

The van was parked by a lagoon, which meant Trevor could fish almost from the van's doorstep. He set up his fishing gear, leaving Martha to give Brian his reward.

Once Brian had scoffed his mince, he wandered over to see Trevor, but was ignored. Trevor was in fishing mode. Still in pyjamas, he was sitting in a chair, watching a fishing rod he had propped in a forked stick. There he waited, hoping for a bite, feeling at peace with the world.

'You can bring me my breakfast now, Martha,' he called, but then the rod tip gave a wiggle. Trevor's muscles tensed. Then the rod gave a bigger wiggle. Trevor leant forward in his chair. Suddenly, the rod flew over the forked stick and was being dragged toward the water. Trevor gave chase, grabbing it just before it disappeared forever. 'I've got one,' he yelled.

Martha came out of the van. 'Why are you standing in the water wearing your pyjamas?' she asked.

Trevor ignored the question. He was fighting a big Carp; his rod almost bent double, the fishing line singing like a violin.

So began the battle, but Trevor could bring the fish no closer than 20-metres from the bank. There it swam in a sweeping arc, first one way, then the other. The impatient angler had to wait for the fish to tire.

Trevor's excitement caught the attention of a passing Pelican. The huge bird landed on the lagoon, its feet acting like water-skis as it touched down. The swoosh was spectacular.

'Look at the beautiful Pelican,' said Martha.

'Can't look now, luv, I need to concentrate on this fish.'

Alas, what happened next would add to Trevor's long list of unfortunate fishing tales. Martha had already told him that birds were smart, but Trevor never suspected that a Pelican could grasp the fundamentals of geometry.

The Pelican placed itself on the 20-metre arc and made ready to ambush Trevor's fish. There it waited for the fish to swim to it, the murky water hiding its crafty plan, the fish's fate almost certain in that shallow lagoon.

Martha saw it all. 'Watch out for the Pelican,' she warned.

'Don't bother me about the Pelican, luv. Can't you see I have a fish on?'

'But, Trev, the Pelican.'

'Forget the Pelican, Martha. Go and fetch the landing net.'

Martha was happy to have reason to leave, for she did not want to witness what was about to happen.

Trevor watched the swirls in the water that told him the position of his fish. Then suddenly, he saw that the swirls and the Pelican were about to meet. *Surely not,* he thought, but his worst fears were realised.

The Pelican speared its beak into the water and Trevor felt the fishing line snap. Then he saw his fish, but it was no longer *his* fish, for it was now struggling in the Pelican's beak.

Martha returned. 'I've got the landing net, Trev.'

'Don't need it now.'

'Did the fish get away, Trev?'

'Not exactly, and now I hate Pelicans.'

'Oh, Trev, did that bad bird get your fish?'

Trevor dropped his fishing rod and turned his back on the water. 'It's time for breakfast, luv,' he mumbled, and then he looked at Brian. 'Come on, Hero. Let's get you some more mince. You're the only bird worth feeding around here.'

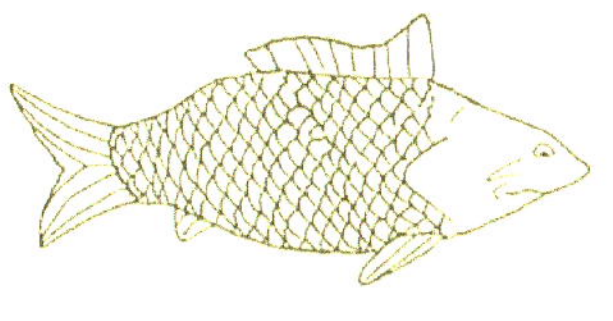

36

CHARLIE GOES TO TOWN

Back at camp, Charlie was preparing for his big day. He had been too nervous to eat breakfast. Instead, he perched himself on a branch that reached out over the water, from where he studied his reflection below. He preened his feathers, checking for dirt. Then he turned his head, first to the left and then to the right, as he decided which was his better side. Next, he let out a loud screech, a less loud screech, a double screech, and finally, a soft screech. He was not sure which of his screeches sounded the most impressive. Max landed beside him.

'What are you doing?' Max asked.

'Nothing.'

'No breakfast this morning?'

'No.'

'Today is your big day. Are you nervous?'

'No.'

'Do you want a wingman?'

'No.'

Charlie had become a bird of few words, for today was the day he would find himself a girlfriend. A wingman could prove useful, but Max was not a romantic. Having him around would spoil any chance of a romantic mood.

Charlie could hear a flock of Cockatoos on the other side of the river and that was where he hoped to find the girl of his dreams. He headed for the Cockatoo chorus, but to his surprise, he found that it came from the nearby town. Charlie wondered why Cockatoos would be in a town when Mother Nature had provided much nicer places to be.

It was a small town consisting of a few houses, some shops, and a police station. A large pine tree stood at its centre, and it was full of noisy Cockatoos that were feeding on pinecones. Charlie landed next to a Cockatoo that was hanging upside down.

'Good morning,' said Charlie. 'My name is Charlie, and this is surely a fine morning to be out.'

The Cockatoo perched upright. 'You're not from these parts, are you?'

'No, I'm from the city, but I think you have a charming little town here.'

'No one has ever called Dog Hill charming before,' remarked the Cockatoo, who was thinking that Charlie was an odd name for someone so well spoken. 'Charlie is short for Charles, I suppose?' he said.

'Oh, that could never be the case,' said Charlie. 'Charles sounds a longer name than Charlie, not a shorter one.'

The Cockatoo screeched, 'Hey, fellers, we have a city boy visiting us today. Let's give him a good, country welcome.'

'Buzz off, city boy.'

'Find your own tree, you toff.'

'We don't want foreigners in our town.'

There were many unkind things said, but the one that upset Charlie the most, was, 'Keep away from our women, you creep.'

Charlie needed to hightail it out of there before the mob got nasty. He took flight, taking refuge in a tree at the far edge of town. There he perched, shattered, as he remembered how his last attempt to join a flock had also ended in failure. He was no different to other Cockatoos, but they always treated him as an outsider. How was he ever going to find a girlfriend if his own people rejected him?

It took Charlie a while to notice that he was in a tree full of almonds, not that he was interested in eating them. Nor was he interested in the house next to the tree or wonder if someone in the house owned the tree. Ownership of a tree was a strange concept to Charlie who thought that Mother Nature owned all the trees.

The man who lived in the house was sitting at his breakfast table. His eldest son looked out the window. 'Hey, Dad, a Cocky has just landed in the almond tree.'

The man stood up. 'Those darn birds. I thought I had taught them all to stay away. I'm getting my shotgun. That thieving scoundrel is about to be blasted to kingdom come.'

Charlie continued to mope in the tree, unaware of the foul deed being planned in his honour. It was while moping that he heard another bird land behind him, but he did not turn around. He could tell that the other bird was a Cockatoo. *The newcomer can eat all the almonds they want*, thought Charlie. He was not hungry.

'You have to get out of this tree, Charlie,' screeched the other Cockatoo.

Charlie thought his harassment would never end. The Cockatoo knew his name, which meant it was one from the flock feeding in the pine tree. They were not giving up until he was gone from their district. But the voice was feminine, and she sounded frantic, not angry. Charlie turned around.

A lady Cockatoo, with a worried look on her face, was perched behind him. Charlie's heart fluttered. She had his full attention, and he failed to notice the back door of the house being quietly opened, but she did.

'Follow me, Charlie, follow me,' she screeched.

But she had no need to repeat her command, for Charlie was ready to follow after hearing it just once. They took off, him hardly noticing the loud boom as they flew away. The shotgun pellets harmlessly passed them by.

37

BELLA

Charlie followed the lady Cockatoo to the other side of the river, where she landed at the top of a dead gum tree. He landed on one of its lower branches. 'Would you mind terribly if I joined you up there?' he asked.

'My, you are such a gentleman. I would be happy for your company.'

Charlie was there in a flash, giving no chance for her to change her mind. But that was the easy part. He had no experience in talking to the opposite sex, and to make matters worse, she was looking for him to start the conversation.

'Aren't all the Cockatoos in your town, gentlemen?' Charlie asked.

She laughed. 'You've met them. They wanted you blasted to bits back there. Now I'm in trouble for saving your life.'

'Thank you for that,' said Charlie.

'My pleasure,' came the reply.

'I'm sorry if I've got you into trouble, though.'

'Think nothing of it. I've always wanted to meet someone from the city, and now I have. That's a big deal for a girl who has spent her whole life stuck in Dog Hill.'

'No boyfriend, no husband?' Charlie asked, tenuously.

'No.'

She had just given the best one-word answer Charlie had ever heard. It was time for him to impress. 'I'm part of the Road Runners gang,' he said, hoping that their fame had spread to Dog Hill.

'I don't think I've heard of them,' she answered. 'What do they do?'

The reply was disappointing, and Charlie was stuck for words. He had no idea why the Humans called them the Road Runners. 'We travel lots,' he said, thinking that to be a lame answer.

'That sounds fantastic,' came the reply. 'I wish I was in your gang.'

'You do?' queried Charlie.

'I would join, but would they have me?'

'Y-yes. I mean yes. Definitely yes. Absolutely yes. I know they will have you.' Charlie was going over the top in saying yes, but he wanted to make sure that she did not think that his answer might have sounded like, 'No.'

His day of near death was suddenly the best day of his life.

The Cockatoos headed back to camp, for Charlie was eager to introduce his lady to the others. Then he remembered something that he might need. It was a minor detail, and Charlie often overlooked minor details. 'What is your name, my dear?' he asked.

Her name was Bella, and Charlie thought that Bella was the nicest name he had ever heard, and she was the nicest person he had ever met. She may not have fared well as a beauty queen, for mites had spoilt her plumage, but to Charlie, Bella was beautiful.

38

FORT FERDINAND

The Road Runners were camped on a river flat, but the place gave Max an eerie feeling, for the trees were all dead. They had once been mighty gums, but were now just skeletons of their former selves, standing in defiance of the evil force that had killed them. Many stood in a shallow lagoon, and the rest stood on the surrounding river flat. Lignum bushes also adorned the flat, so tangled in places that only the most stubborn of creatures would ever bother to push through them.

It was a place like nothing Max could ever have imagined, had he not seen it for himself. Trees growing in a lagoon seemed an impossibility, but the evidence was there for all to see. In one place, the Humans had cut a narrow track that led to a clearing. This was where Trevor and Martha were camped.

Max's task that day was to find a hiding place for Snowy, and the far side of the lagoon looked ideal. It was a place that could only be reached by a creature capable of bounding over the lignums, and Kangaroos were the only bounding creatures Max knew.

He crossed the lagoon, resting at times on the dead trees that stood in the water. On the far bank, he spied another Magpie, perched high above the ground. Finding a fellow Magpie was something unexpected, and so he landed on the dead tree where the Magpie was perched.

'Halt, who goes there?' squawked the perched Magpie.

'Who goes where?' Max asked.

The challenging Magpie continued. 'Tell me your name, stranger.'

'Max.'

'And what business does Max have at the Fortress of Ferdinand?'

'The fortress of who?'

'Ferdinand. He is our leader. Why do you trespass at his fort?'

Max was puzzled. If Ferdinand was the leader, then the place should be called the Kingdom of Ferdinand. Max thought that he was the only Magpie leader ever to break with tradition. He had decreed that his kingdom would retain its Human name of Eden Springs. A fellow tradition breaker was a Magpie Max wanted to meet. 'Take me to your leader,' he squawked.

The challenging Magpie took a deep breath and warbled a most impressive warble. 'Magpie Max seeks an audience with the mighty Ferdinand.' He was looking down as he made the announcement.

Below was a clearing in the lignums, in which a group of Kangaroos lounged on bare ground. Upon hearing the Magpie's warble, they stood to attention and formed a circle. The tallest of the Kangaroos looked up and nodded. 'He may enter the fortress.'

'Where am I supposed to be entering?' Max asked.

The challenging Magpie put a wing to the side of his beak and whispered, 'Just go and talk to the big Kangaroo, Dumbo.'

Max could not remember the last time someone had called him Dumbo. He thought city boy was the preferred insult in that part of the world.

He landed in the circle of Kangaroos and looked about, but there were no Magpies. He saw only the Kangaroos and some Rabbits dozing under the lignums.

The tall Kangaroo frowned, and then he spoke. 'Well?'

'Well, what?' replied Max.

'Why do you seek my audience?'

'Are you Ferdinand?'

'Commander Ferdinand if you don't mind.'

'You're Commander Ferdinand?'

'Has anyone ever called you Dumbo?' asked the commander. 'I just told you who I am. Now state your business.'

Max heard a snigger come from the Magpie in the dead tree.

'Is this your fort?' Max asked, thinking the question would earn him whatever insult came after Dumbo, but Ferdinand's attitude changed.

'This place is sanctuary for the hunted and homeless,' said Ferdinand. 'Only Kangaroos can reach this place, for only they can bound over the lignums that keep our enemies at bay.' A small cough came from beneath the lignums. 'Oh yes, the Bunnies get here by running under the bushes.'

'What about Magpies?' Max asked.

'Of course, Magpies can fly here,' scoffed Ferdinand. 'We owe much to our Magpie friends. They stand guard on our watchtower. You have only been granted an audience because you are a Magpie. Now state your business.'

'I'm trying to find a safe hiding place for my Kangaroo friend, Snowy.'

Ferdinand raised his eyebrows. 'Snowy, the albino?' he asked.

'Yes,' said Max.

A collective gasp came from the circle of Kangaroos, and Ferdinand's ears began to twitch.

'Not Australia's Most Wanted?'

'That's what he tells us.'

Ferdinand fixed a wistful gaze to the sky and launched into another inspiring speech.

'This mob has wreaked havoc for generations. We leave this place each night and raid the crops of the Humans, but they can never catch us. The lignums, the mud, and the creeks, foil their hunting dogs. We have had many glorious warriors in our past, but none so famous as Australia's Most Wanted. Do you think we could possibly meet the famous Snowy?'

'My guess is that Snowy might want to join your raiders,' Max replied.

Another collective gasp came from the surrounding Kangaroos, causing Max to wonder if collective gasping was something they practiced. They were so good at it.

Ferdinand stooped to shake Max's wing. 'Your visit to us is indeed most welcome, Mr Max. Any friend of Australia's Most Wanted is a friend of ours. We would be most honoured if you could introduce us to your famous associate.'

Max had found the ultimate sanctuary for a Kangaroo, but then he wondered about the Rabbits. 'Are the Rabbits also hunted and homeless?' he asked.

Ferdinand smiled. 'The Bunnies are indeed hunted,' he said, 'but they have a home. They only visit us when their water supply goes dry. They say our dead gums remind them of their ballerina tree back home.'

The lights flashed in Max's detective brain. He had found Tripod's family, although they would know him as Ralph. 'Do any of you know a small Bunny called Ralph?' he asked the Rabbits.

'We all do,' was their collective reply. It seemed that collective speaking was something everyone practiced at the fort.

'I will bring both Snowy and Ralph here,' Max announced. 'We found them both on our travels.'

A mother Rabbit turned to her husband. 'This wonderful Magpie has found our boy, Arthur, and he is going to bring him home to us.'

'Hooray,' shouted the Rabbits, again, all as one.

Ferdinand laughed. 'You have done well, Mr Max. It looks like you will be killing two birds with the one stone.'

Max hastened away, for it would take the rest of the day to bring back Snowy and Tripod. It had been a worthwhile visit, despite the commander's lack of political correctness. *Killing two birds with the one stone,* was a saying frowned upon in Max's world, but he knew the commander meant no harm by it.

WISDOM AND KNOWLEDGE

Of all those leaving camp that morning, Alice was the most excited. She had dreamt of this day ever since Nebbie had told her about the Great River, the place where Mother Nature's creatures gathered to exchange wisdom and knowledge. Alice had searched for the river after her father kicked her out, but never did she imagine that not only would she reach the river one day, but that her father would be with her when she did.

Albert and Bernard had both asked Alice if they could join her that morning. Alice had never been close to her dad, but he had become a more normal person since that horrible day when he tried to kill her. Having him by her side now was like a dream come true.

The three Magpies headed for the river, but then Alice faltered. She began having doubts, for she was just a simple girl with no wisdom and knowledge to exchange. Sure, there had been a time when she was the famous Dove Girl, but the dive Dopey taught her was not wisdom and knowledge. Nebbie's tutoring was also of no use because he only talked about the Great River, and everybody here knew about that.

Alice thought about her journey to get to where she was, but that was not wisdom and knowledge. She thought about Colin, the boy in a wheelchair. She could make Colin laugh, but that was not wisdom and knowledge. She had no wisdom and knowledge to exchange. In fact, she was not even sure what wisdom and knowledge was.

Her excitement melted into an ocean of self-doubt, and she landed in a small tree. Albert and Bernard landed beside her. They looked at her, waiting for her to speak.

'What is wisdom and knowledge, and what am I here to find, and what can I tell them that they don't already know?' Alice blurted it all out, and her dad was not sure how to answer, but Bernard put a wing on her shoulder. He spoke softly.

'All you lack is confidence, my girl. Only you know what you know, and sometimes it can be wisest to say nothing at all. Wisdom does not come in a single day, it comes with experience, and no other Magpie has experienced what you have experienced. You have much wisdom and knowledge to share. I suggest you let an old confidence trickster like me, give you some help.'

Alice had disliked Bernard ever since the day he had thrown her into the wilderness, but she was now seeing some good qualities in her father's newfound friend.

They took off once more, hoping to find a bird that looked wise, and they came upon a Pelican swimming on the river. Alice thought that a Pelican might be wise because she had seen Pelicans circling high in the sky. A Pelican would see everything, but she had a problem.

The Pelican was swimming on the river, but she was standing on the bank. If she were a Duck, she could swim out and begin a casual conversation, but Magpie's do not swim. Her doubts returned. How was she going to meet people if she could not swim? Bernard came to her rescue. 'Hey, Mr Pelican, come in here,' he squawked.

The Pelican swam to the bank and waddled up to them. He looked huge on land.

'My friend, Alice, wants to ask you some questions,' said Bernard.

Alice felt uncomfortable with Bernard's abrupt approach, but the Pelican seemed unfazed. He looked at Alice with soft, dark eyes that peered down a very long beak. He seemed friendly. 'What would you like to know, young lady?' he asked.

'I have come here seeking wisdom and knowledge. Can you tell me where I can find it?' Alice's voice was full of uncertainty.

'Everyone here wants the answer to that question,' laughed the Pelican. 'I can only tell you how to catch fish.'

'But you must have travelled,' Bernard interrupted.

'Yes,' said the Pelican. 'I have travelled from the ocean to the middle of Australia.'

'Tell us about the middle of Australia,' said Bernard, 'and Alice will tell you about life in the city.'

The Pelican squatted on the ground and so began a morning that Alice would never forget. The warmth of the sun, the sounds of the river, it was all so magical. She could hear birds of unknown type, calling from places she could not see. The still of the river gave each call a mystical sound. Alice had never known a place so peaceful, and amid it all, she was exchanging wisdom and knowledge.

When the Pelican left, Bernard asked her what she had learnt. Alice thought a moment. She had learnt what it was like to fly to the middle of Australia, and she had told the Pelican about life in the city. 'I think we all have wisdom and knowledge to share,' she said, 'but we just don't know it.'

40

WHAT'S IN A NAME

Not everyone left camp that morning. The ground crew stayed, as did the rest of the Magpie girls. Grandma could not be bothered searching for wisdom and knowledge. Garry asked her, 'Why not?'

'No more room,' said Grandma. 'My brain is full already.'

Garry laughed. 'You forget so many things these days, Grandma. Your head must have lots of empty spaces.'

Lofty sprang to Grandma's defence. 'I cannot remember a single thing that Grandma has forgotten.'

'That's because you are the world's most forgetful Emu,' said Garry.

'Am I?'

Garry rolled his eyes. 'The only person with a good memory around here is me.'

'Then why aren't you out searching for wisdom and knowledge?' asked Grandma.

'Already know it all,' said Garry.

'Me too,' said Lofty.

'You too, what?' growled Garry.

'Me too, whatever we are talking about.'

'Can't remember, can you?'

'I think we were talking about that bird over there.'

Lofty was looking at a bird that had just landed on a fallen branch. The bird looked interesting, and so he walked over to have a chat.

Garry looked at Grandma. 'Lofty is off with the fairies again. It's hard to have a normal conversation with him these days.'

'Have you two ever had a normal conversation?' asked Grandma.

'Short ones, Grandma. Very short ones.'

Garry walked over to join Lofty and the bird.

'Garry, meet my new friend. He's a Cormorant,' said Lofty.

'No, he's not. He's a Shag. Trailblazer told me that this morning.'

'You're a Cormorant, aren't you, Mr Cormorant?' Lofty asked.

'I most certainly am,' said the Cormorant. 'Cormorants hate being called Shags.'

'Shag,' taunted Garry.

'Cormorant,' said the Cormorant.

'Shag.'

'Cormorant.'

'Next thing, you will be calling yourself a Penguin,' laughed Garry.

Max had once told Garry about Penguins, but Garry was convinced that Max had made them up.

'A Penguin?' queried the Cormorant.

'Yes, a Penguin,' said Garry. 'Penguins live in a land of ice, but like Cormorants, they don't actually exist.'

'Penguins do exist,' said the Cormorant. 'There are small ones living near the mouth of this river and the bigger ones live in the land of ice.'

'I don't believe you,' said Garry, 'so get lost.'

'People should call you Grumpy,' laughed the Cormorant as he flew away.

Grandma turned to Muriel. 'I think that Cormorant is a lot smarter than Garry gives him credit for. Perhaps there is truth in the story about Penguins after all.'

41

A NEW ADVENTURE

As planned, the Road Runners gathered back at camp in the late afternoon. Only Brian was absent. He had spent the day with Trevor and Martha and was hoping for more treats before leaving.

Each Road Runner gave a report on what they had done that day, and all were delighted to hear that Snowy had joined Ferdinand's raiders and Tripod was back with his family. But it was the Pigeon's report that drew the most interest. They had flown to the river mouth and back.

'Wow,' said Alice, 'you have to tell us what you saw.'

'Tell Garry about the Penguins living there,' said Lofty.

'Quiet,' scowled Garry.

'What's this about Penguins?' asked Max.

Max had avoided the subject of Penguins since first telling Garry about them, for it had left Garry thinking that Max harboured some very strange beliefs. Apparently, telling people you believe in a race of flightless birds that lived in a land of ice and swam like fish, was not a good idea. But now it seemed that Lofty knew something about them.

Lofty began his answer. 'Garry had an argument with a Cormorant and—'

Garry pushed Lofty aside. 'It was a Shag, not a Cormorant.'

Lofty kicked Garry in the butt. 'Cormorant,' he snorted.

'Shag,' said Garry as he stomped on Lofty's foot.

'Ouch,' cried Lofty.

'Settle down you two,' said Max, 'Let's just call it a bird. Lofty, please tell us your story.'

'The Cormorant said Penguins live near the mouth of the river.'

Garry's temper rose. 'Lofty, how come you can never remember what I tell you, but you can remember what that stupid Shag had to say?'

Max had always wondered about Nebbie's fanciful Penguin story. It was the only Nebbie story for which there was no proof. Nebbie had said that Max should consider becoming a scientist. *What if I can prove the existence of Penguins,* thought Max. *That would make me the greatest scientist of all.* 'Who's in favour of flying to the river mouth to look for a Penguin?' he squawked.

'I will go,' said Alice. 'If the Pigeons can fly there, then we can do it too.'

The vote was unanimous, but then Garry saw a problem. 'Lofty and I can't fly,' he said.

'Not a problem,' said Bernard. 'Who's in favour of leaving Garry and Lofty behind?' He raised his wing.

'They might kill each other while we are gone,' Alice giggled.

'That's a risk I'm willing to take,' laughed Bernard.

Garry's head dropped, but Lofty was preoccupied. He was wondering why his foot hurt, having already forgotten that Garry had stomped on it.

Bernard felt a touch of guilt. 'Only kidding,' he said.

'But Bernard is right,' said Trailblazer. 'It would take many days for the ground crew to get to the river mouth, but the rest of you could fly there in three.'

It was then that Brian returned to camp. He had missed his chance to vote, not that it mattered. They never counted his vote anyway. But when Max told him that they were going to the mouth of the river and he was coming with them, Brian became unexpectedly defiant. 'I'm staying here, and from now on, my name is Hero.'

'What did you just say?' Max asked.

'My new name is Hero. That is what the Humans call me.'

Muriel put her wing over Alice's beak to stop her from giggling.

'I think he is serious,' said Max.

Brian continued. 'I am not going anywhere. I am staying here with my new friends, Trevor and Martha. They call me Hero.'

'Brian, you are coming with us,' Albert growled.

'No, Dad, I'm going to live with Trevor and Martha. Humans know how to treat a Magpie.'

Albert thought he would never see the day that his favourite son would defy him, but somehow, he took it better than expected.

Bernard slapped Albert on the back. 'Brian might be a chip off the old block after all,' he chuckled.

42

FAMILY UNITY

There was excitement among the flyers next morning, and only the ground crew noticed the morning chorus sounding different. 'Hey, Mr Choir Master, I think you have lost a member,' said Garry.

Albert took a headcount. Brian was missing for the second day in a row. 'Where is Brian?' he squawked.

'Who cares?' said Max. 'Brian said he wasn't coming with us. We should just go and leave him here.'

'We can't do that,' squawked Albert. 'Brian thinks he can survive in the real world without us, but he can't.'

'Your dad is right,' added Muriel. 'We have to find him.'

But then Brian appeared.

'Where have you been?' asked Muriel.

Brian was sobbing. 'Mum, their caravan has gone. They must have left last night, and they went without me.'

Albert put a wing on Brian's shoulder. 'Don't worry, son. You have just learnt a valuable lesson. Humans cannot be trusted, but you can always rely on family.'

'Albert is a wonderful father,' said Penelope.

Max looked at Alice, for neither could believe what Penelope had just said. Albert had been a horrible father to them. His violence had caused them both to leave home, but they could see that he had become more tolerant since then.

Muriel joined Albert in comforting Brian, causing Max to feel a little ashamed. He looked at Brian. 'Do you want to come with us?' he asked, but then Garry interrupted.

'No, Brian. Stay with me. We can take it in turns to look after Lofty.'

Brian stopped sobbing and thought about Garry's offer. 'No thanks,' he said. 'I think I will stay with my family.'

'Good for you,' Max cheered. 'Our family should always stick together.' He was hoping that his sudden change of attitude toward Brian would make up for his uncaring *who cares* comment he had made that morning.

As everyone was now ready to go, they spread their wings and took to the sky. Trailblazer led the way.

'Goodbye, Garry and Lofty,' they shouted.

'Don't fly too fast or you will wear out Grandma,' Garry bleated.

'Where are they going?' said a puzzled Lofty.

'Nowhere special,' said Garry. 'They will be back in a few days.'

43

A FREE RIDE

The flock's first stop was to forage for breakfast, during which Alice asked Trailblazer a question. 'Why do they call it the mouth of the river?'

'It is called the mouth of the river because that is where the water runs into the sea,' Trailblazer explained.

'In that case, it should be called the mouth of the sea,' said Alice. Then she paused, for she had never heard of a thing called the sea. She began to imagine a massive monster slurping up the river's water. 'How big is the sea and what does it do?' she asked.

Trailblazer was discovering the reason Max could never win an argument with his sister. She had a way of twisting things around and then asking a confusing question. He decided to respond by giving her an equally confusing answer. 'The sea is so big that its end has never been found,' he said, 'and it keeps for itself, the water it drinks and the land that it covers.'

Alice could not picture this thing called the sea, but now she was worried. Water and land were Mother Nature's greatest gifts, yet the sea was robbing her creatures of both. 'Trailblazer, you are leading us to a place where a thing of evil is at war with Mother Nature,' she said.

'Perhaps,' said Trailblazer. 'You will just have to wait and see.'

The flock continued their journey, but then they came to another place where war was being waged against Mother Nature.

Max hated how Humans built fences on land, but he never expected to find one built across the river. A wall was holding back the water.

Max went into detective mode, for he realised that before him was a murder weapon, used in the crime that troubled him. The wall was causing water to flood the river flat, creating a lagoon and drowning the trees. This undeniable evidence was proof that the Humans were tree murderers, for the wall was theirs. He closed the case of *Who Killed the Trees*.

Later that morning, Grandma asked a question normally left to a younger generation. 'Are we there yet?'

'Not even close,' said Trailblazer.

'That's too bad,' said Grandma, 'because I feel pooped.'

She looked about and saw a log drifting along in the current. It appeared to have a mast in the form of a single branch that pointed skyward. A Cormorant was perched on the mast.

'That Cormorant has the right idea,' said Grandma. 'I think we should capture his vessel.'

Max agreed, for Grandma needed to rest. He pointed to the log. 'Prepare for boarding,' he squawked, and the flock swooped in formation.

The Cormorant had been dozing, but then he sensed that something was wrong. He looked up. An assortment of birds was bearing down on him, and many questions ran through his mind. *What have I done? When was war declared? Is this an invasion?* He was not sure if he was dreaming or awake, but either way, he was getting off that log. With wings slapping the water, he strained to become airborne. 'I need to find safe harbour,' he mumbled. 'This place has become a hunting ground for pirates.'

The flock landed on the log and were soon enjoying a river cruise. 'You know,' said Max, 'this journey could take a little longer than planned.' They were discovering the serenity that comes when you simply drift along with the world passing you by.

But the serenity was soon broken, for they could hear a roar coming from somewhere ahead. The sound became louder, for it was getting closer. Suddenly, a boat came hurtling around the bend, a plume of spray rising from its side. Everyone gasped at how fast the boat was going, but what followed left them stunned.

Two Humans were trying to catch the boat. They had managed to snare it with ropes but still needed to give chase. The flock gasped, for the Humans had superpowers. They were standing on the water, defying one of Mother Nature's most basic laws.

'Those are the scariest Humans I have ever seen,' said Grandma.

Everyone agreed, and they watched in shock as the boat disappeared upriver.

'We're safe now,' said Max, but then the boat's wake hit them. Everyone hung on as the log began to rock.

'What do you mean *safe*?' squawked Brian. 'Those Humans are trying to drown us. We're all going to die.' He abandoned ship and headed for the safety of dry land.

Bella was perched at the top of the mast, and everyone heard a loud splosh as she fell into the water.

'Bernard, dive in and save her,' Max squawked.

'Why me?'

'You're closest.'

'Can't swim.'

'None of us can swim.'

Charlie realised that it was up to him to save his newfound sweetheart.

'I'm coming, my love,' he screeched, not realising until too late, that Bella was already scrambling back on board.

'Thanks for the rescue, boys,' she gibed as she plopped onto the log. A second splosh then happened behind her. She turned to investigate. Charlie had just performed a spectacular bellyflop.

'What are you doing in the water?' she yelled.

'Rescuing—cough—you, my love.'

'Get back on the log, you duffer.'

Charlie completed his own rescue the same as had Bella.

The rest of the day was enjoyed by all, as they relaxed in the warmth of the sun. Only Brian had a problem. He returned, but then complained of feeling seasick.

Come evening, they went ashore to roost. Their adventure on the high seas was over, and they could but wave their trusty vessel goodbye, as it continued its journey without them.

44

THE DEFECTION OF BRIAN

The river was truly a wondrous place, and the flock was meeting birds of every kind. Some were fat, some thin, some coloured, some plain, some with long legs, and some with short. But there was one bird that Max had yet to meet, and he wondered if any still existed. Nebbie had told him how the Sparrows had fled the invasion of the Noisy Miners, and he did not know if any survived. Max was beginning to wonder the same thing.

At times, he would ask a bird if they had met a Sparrow, but none had. But he never asked if any had met a Penguin. He feared ridicule if he said he believed in them.

The river was also a place where Humans did strange things, and day two of their travels revealed something almost as weird as standing on water.

Despite there being an abundance of land on which to build a house, Humans were building them on boats. Added to this, they were putting wheels on the boats. Putting wheels on a car seemed a good idea, but wheels on a boat made no sense at all. One boat was particularly noteworthy.

It was a very large boat on which stood a very large house, and at the back was a wheel that churned the water. Humans sat around the house, all soaking up the sun in their deck chairs. They appeared to be enjoying a river cruise, but typical of their species, they needed more comfort than could be provided by a log.

Later that morning, the flock came upon another surprise. Trevor and Martha's caravan was parked on the riverbank. Brian gave a squawk and was gone. The rest followed. They perched in a tree above the van and watched Brian as he knocked on the door.

Trevor lifted his head from the newspaper. 'Don't know who that could be, luv. We don't know anyone around here. You'd better see who it is.'

Martha put down her knitting and went to the door. She looked out, saw nobody, and went back to her knitting. 'Nobody there, Trev.'

'Don't be silly, Martha. Someone just knocked.'

Trevor got up, opened the door, and he also saw nobody. But then he stepped forward and tripped over Brian. Brian dashed under the caravan, not wanting to be blamed for Trevor's stumble. Alice began to giggle but stopped when her mother poked her in the ribs.

'What happened, Trev?' called Martha.

'I must have tripped over my feet, luv.'

Brian popped out from under the van. His involvement in Trevor's mishap had gone undetected.

Trevor looked in disbelief. 'Martha, I think little Hero is back.'

'How would you know, Trev? All Magpies look alike.'

'This one was under our van.'

'Do you really think we have a Magpie living under our caravan, Trev?'

'Maybe.'

'Trevor, please don't tell anyone else that story. They might start to worry about you.'

But Trevor was convinced, even if he could not explain how Hero would find them for a third time. 'Come here, Hero,' he said. 'Uncle Trevor will get you some mince.'

Brian squawked to the flock. 'See, my name is Hero. That is what people call me now.'

'I feel ill,' Alice mumbled.

'Me too,' said Max.

'Time to gate-crash the party,' said Bernard.

Trevor soon discovered that he had many mouths to feed, but he was delighted.

'Look, Martha, I have proof it is Hero because he has that weird collection of birds with him.'

Max turned to Mayzie. 'We aren't weird, are we?', but Mayzie chose not to answer.

'Bring out the bread and the biscuits,' said Trevor, and so began a party. But the mood changed when it came time to leave, for Brian declared that he was staying.

'Brian, you're coming with us,' growled Albert.

'My name is Hero, and I am staying here.'

The flock began to mumble between themselves. No one liked the idea of calling him Hero. Bernard had a quiet word in Albert's ear. 'If Brian no longer wants to be known by the name you gave him, and if he no longer wants to be one of us, then we should let him go. No one wants to call him Hero.'

Reluctantly, Albert agreed. He shook Brian by the wing and his mother pecked him on the beak.

'Goodbye, Brian,' said his siblings, neither moving from where they were perched.

Later that day, Trevor came out with more food, but he only found Brian. The rest were gone.

45

THE SOUND OF EVIL

Albert flew on with heavy heart. He had always looked forward to the day that he could throw out his children, but Brian had been different. He thought they had a special bond, but that bond had been broken. He was struggling to accept what had happened.

Grandma was also struggling. Mayzie was flying beside her, making sure she was not left behind. Finally, Grandma could fly no more.

'Please tell Max we have to stop,' she puffed.

'Okay,' said Mayzie. 'I guess Max won't mind.'

'Tell Max I will haunt him forever if too much flying kills me.'

Mayzie flew ahead to give Max the message. 'Max, we have to stop.'

'Why.'

'Grandma has something bad planned for you if we don't.'

Getting on the wrong side of Grandma was something Max always avoided, but ahead was something that could solve the problem. The log had continued its journey throughout the night and was waiting to take them back on board.

With squawks of delight, they landed on their river cruiser, but no one risked perching on its mast. Grandma found a comfortable spot to doze, while the rest enjoyed the ever-changing scenery. That evening, they dined on the riverbank's finest cuisine and found lodgings in the trees. Darkness fell and silence followed, but then something began to puzzle them.

Coming from the direction of their destination, was a faint, distant rumble. Max thought it might be the drone of a city, but there was no glow in the sky. At times, they would hear it, but then it would fade. Come sunrise, it was gone, lost in the morning breeze.

Max was eager to get going again. 'Is everyone ready?' he said.

'No,' squawked Grandma. She was perched on the same branch that she had landed on the night before. 'I'm too sore to go anywhere,' she said.

Max did not know what to do, but Charlie came to his rescue. 'Bella and I can stay with Grandma until you get back,' he said.

Charlie's offer was prompted by an ulterior motive, for he was concerned that too much flying might cause Bella to reconsider her Road Runner membership. But Max saw no such motive in the offer.

'Three cheers for Charlie,' he cried. 'He is prepared to take one for the team.'

Everyone cheered, and Charlie responded with a modest thank you.

The flock left Grandma with the Cockatoos, saying they would be back in a couple of days. They took to the air, but paused their journey mid-morning, for they could now hear the mystery sound on the breeze. Alice began to worry, for Trailblazer had given her concerns about their destination.

'What is that sound?' she asked him.

'You might worry if I tell you,' he laughed.

'Why,'

'It is the sound of evil,' he whispered.

'MAX!' squawked Alice. 'Trailblazer said he is taking us to a place of evil.'

'Is this true?' Max asked.

'Nothing to worry about,' said Trailblazer. 'It's just a little joke I'm having with Alice.'

Max never knew what to make of Pigeon humour, but Trailblazer could be annoying at times. 'Don't worry,' he said to Alice. 'We are Magpies, and Magpies never run from danger.'

They flew on, but then came to a place where the river flowed into a vast lake. Alice's heart began to race. 'Trailblazer, we have come to the end of the river. Where is the monster that drinks it?'

Trailblazer laughed. 'This is only a lake. The mouth is on the other side. That is where the sea drinks the river. The sea is the sound you have been hearing.'

Alice was afraid to go further. 'I'm going to ask Max to turn back,' she said.

'Please don't,' said Trailblazer. 'Tomorrow, you will see the end of the world as you know it. You wouldn't want to miss seeing the end of the world, would you?'

Trailblazer had gone too far. He was telling her either that the world would end tomorrow, or that they were coming to where the world ends. If it were the first, he would be worried. It had to be the second.

To come to the end of the world was worth meeting a monster. She had already faced the Great Gandor, and that meeting had turned out rather well. Max was right. They were Magpies and Magpies don't turn their back on danger. 'Okay, Trailblazer,' she said. 'Tomorrow, I expect you to show me the end of the world. Don't let me down.'

46

THE BATTLE OF GOOD AND EVIL

The scenery around the lake was different to that of the river. Instead of gums and willows, they were now seeing bushes and fences, scattered across a carpet of lush, green grass.

As the lake was far too wide for a Magpie to cross, they set out along its shore. In the distance was a row of sand dunes, which they reached not long before dark. By then, the wind had begun to howl, so they made camp in the shelter of the dunes.

The mystery sound was now close, for they could hear it above the howl of the wind. Max guessed it was coming from just beyond the dunes, so he flew to the top of one to investigate. There, the sound seemed to explode before him, but when he looked toward it, sand blasted in his face.

'What is making that sound?' Alice asked when he returned.

'Couldn't see a thing,' said Max. 'The air up there is filled with swirling grit.'

'Trailblazer, tell us what the noise is,' Alice demanded.

'I have already told you,' he said.

'You said it was the sound of evil.'

'Don't worry,' Max interrupted. 'Trailblazer is still here. The Pigeons would be gone if we were in danger.'

The roar of evil was in Alice's ears, and that same evil had just blasted Max with grit. Her doubts returned, and she felt like shouting, *we are all going to die*, but that was something Brian would do. She looked at the others, but no one seemed to share her concern. *Oh well,* she thought. *If something evil gets us, at least we die together.*

The morning came and the wind was gone, but the evil sound remained, and Max could not wait to see what it was. 'Is everyone ready to go?' he asked, but Alice wanted to delay things a little longer.

'Let's have breakfast first,' she said. 'I don't want to die with an empty stomach.'

'Good idea,' said Bernard. 'Who's for having breakfast?'

Max was the only one to vote against the suggestion, so the rest went off and foraged in some grass. He thought about leaving them there, but that was not what a good leader does, so he joined them for breakfast.

With breakfast over, Alice came up with an even better stalling tactic. 'I suggest that Trailblazer scouts ahead and reports if danger lurks beyond the dunes,' she said.

'Not a problem,' said Trailblazer. He departed and Penelope followed.

Bernard chuckled as the Pigeons disappeared. 'I hope Alice hasn't sent them to their doom,' he said.

'I hope so too,' said Alice. 'I want to know what is making that sound.'

The Pigeons returned. 'I have no danger to report,' announced Trailblazer.

'So, what is the evil sound?' said Alice.

Trailblazer laughed. 'Follow me, for yonder lies the end of our world.'

The flock took off with Alice trailing a short distance behind. She was last to land at the top of the dunes, but when she did, she gasped.

Below was a beach and beyond that was the sea, and between the two was thundering surf. That was the sound they were hearing.

Alice watched the waves, one behind the other, each becoming a wall of water as it neared the shore. To her, they seemed like mighty warriors, each casting a cloak of spray as they charged upon the land. But then, when almost ready to strike, they would collapse, and harmless foam would spill onto the beach.

Trailblazer said that the sea drank the rivers, but it appeared to want more. It was trying to eat the land as well, but Mother Nature would not let it. She was commanding the waves to die before they could fulfill their mission.

This field of battle was the most breathtaking scene Alice had ever witnessed. Mother Nature ruled both land and sea, and evil was being defeated.

47

SOME DOGS ARE DIFFERENT

It was while gazing at the sea, that they noticed something odd on the beach. A dark lump they thought to be a rock, let out a bark. The bark could be heard above the noise of the surf, and it had Max excited. The discovery of a barking rock would rank even greater than finding a Penguin. The flock flew down for a closer inspection, but disappointment followed. It was only a dog. The dog was lying on the beach, staring at the dunes. He briefly turned his head as they arrived, and then resumed what he was doing. 'Stupid dog,' said Max. 'Let's go. We need to find a Penguin.'

'I don't think the dog can hear us,' said Penelope. 'The poor thing has such tiny ears.'

Everyone agreed that they were the tiniest ears they had ever seen on a dog, but not everyone shared Penelope's sympathy.

Bernard disliked dogs, and the opportunity to insult one that could not hear, was too good to pass up. 'Hey, Mr Dog,' he said. 'Has anyone ever told you that you have a weird head, but I guess you don't hear what they say?'

'Beat it,' barked the dog.

'The dog speaks,' squawked Bernard.

'Scram, I'm hunting.'

'What are you hunting?'

'Tricky little fairies, so get lost.'

'You're hunting fairies,' scoffed Bernard. 'That's very brave of you. Aren't you afraid that they might beat you to death with their little fairy wands?'

The dog lunged at Bernard but stumbled because he had no legs. Bernard could not believe his luck. All his life, he had wanted to swoop a dog but could never muster the courage. Coming across a dog with no legs was an opportunity too good to miss. It was time for him to fulfil his ambition.

'You need to learn that Magpies don't like dogs chasing them,' he squawked, and he swooped his startled victim.

Albert joined the attack, and Max was thinking about doing the same, but Alice held him back. 'I'm here to find wisdom and knowledge,' she growled. 'How can I do that if you fight everyone we meet?'

'And you are here to find a Penguin,' Mayzie added, 'and that dog probably knows where they live.'

Unfortunately, Bernard and Albert had done the damage, for the strange dog was not staying to answer questions. He headed for the water, which was when everyone noticed that he had flippers where legs should have been. The flippers made him awkward on land, but once in the water, he swam like a fish.

The dog swam out beyond the breakers and then surfed back to shore. 'I bet you wish you could do what us Seals can do?' he barked as he turned back out to sea.

The creature had called himself a Seal and he liked to show off. Max was impressed. 'I wish I could swim like that,' he said.

'I don't,' said Alice. 'I think that silly Seal is jealous of us.'

'How could we make him jealous?' Max asked.

Alice laughed. 'We know how to fly.'

48

PENGUIN PETE

Max called his troops to order. 'We are here to find a Penguin, not fight the locals,' he squawked, but Bernard wanted to argue.

'Max, I think your Penguin is a joke. Mother Nature would never make a bird with flippers instead of wings.'

Max disagreed. 'We have arrived at the end of the world where creatures are probably different. If a dog can have flippers, then why not a bird?'

'Where is the ice?' said Bernard. 'You said that Penguins live in a land of ice. How could such a place exist?'

A voice came from behind. 'Those Penguins are my cousins. They are the ones who live in a land of ice.'

Everyone spun around. A bird, about the size of a Magpie, came out from the dunes and waddled toward them. 'Thanks for getting rid of that Seal,' honked the bird. 'He was out to get me.'

The bird walked upright, but instead of wings, it had flippers.

Bernard went quiet.

'Are the Penguins your cousins?' asked Max.

'Yes, and I'm a Penguin too,' honked the bird. 'I'm a Fairy Penguin, but you can call me Pete. My cousins are bigger than me.'

Max was stunned by the enormity of the occasion. They had just made a great discovery that would benefit Magpie Science. No more would he be embarrassed to talk about Penguins and their land of ice.

'Where is the land of ice?' asked Alice.

'On the other side of the sea,' said Pete.

'You mean we are not at the end of the world?' Alice replied.

'There is no end to the world,' Pete exclaimed.

Alice could not imagine how the world could go on forever, but Nebbie had once told her much the same thing. *Will I ever have enough wisdom and knowledge to understand everything,* she wondered.

145

Pete told them that he was about to have breakfast when the Seal chased him onto the beach, and the chase had caused Pete to strain his leg. The injury was now slowing him down. 'The Seal will be waiting for me,' he said. 'If I try to swim back home, he knows he can catch me.'

'Where is your home?' Max asked.

Pete pointed to a small island just off the end of the beach. 'On there,' he said.

'I don't see any trees on that island,' said Max. 'Where do Penguins build their nests?'

'We live under the rocks,' said Pete. 'The island is our rookery.'

Max suggested that Pete walk along the beach with the flock acting as bodyguards. They could swoop the Seal if it tried to come ashore.

'I don't think I can walk that far,' said Pete. 'I could try swimming, but the Seal will probably get me.'

'What if you swim close to the beach and come ashore if the Seal tries anything,' said Max.

'Good plan,' Bernard added. 'It will give me great pleasure to swoop that mongrel again.'

Pete agreed to the idea and began swimming close in, with the odd wave washing him back onto the beach. Meanwhile, the Seal stayed behind the breakers, but occasionally came close. Each time, the Magpies squawked the alarm until the Seal finally gave up. He swam away.

They continued towards Pete's home until coming upon something unusual. A flock of clean, white birds was watching a group of Humans haul in a net.

'Look at those birds,' said Alice. 'They seem so gentle, just standing there, bothering no one.'

'That is how every flock should behave,' said Max. 'Those birds are a picture of law and order.'

'They are Seagulls,' laughed Trailblazer. 'We should stay and watch the fun.'

Max was not sure what Trailblazer meant, but fun was something he liked to watch. They perched on a boat the Humans had pulled on to the beach, and Pete joined them. 'I could do with a feed of fish,' he said. 'I missed out on breakfast this morning.'

Max did not know why Pete would raise the subject of fish, but he soon found out. The Humans pulled the last of the net out of the water and it was full of fish. Chaos erupted. The Humans were grabbing large fish and throwing them into the boat while the Seagulls pounced on the smaller ones.

Max's flock was surrounded by the biggest bird brawl they had ever seen. Bad language filled the air as Gulls went on a rampage of tug-of-war and peck-thy-neighbour. There were no rules. A victorious Gull would take to the air with a fish in its beak and then be attacked by another. The fish would drop, and the fight for it would begin again.

'I would love some of those little fish,' said Pete.

'Don't expect us to fight that mob,' laughed Bernard.

'We don't have to fight the Gulls on the beach,' said Max. 'We can fight them in the air.'

The Magpies joined the aerial chase, adding more confusion to an already confusing contest. Pete soon had more fish than he could eat, while the Magpies were discovering a new sport at which they excelled.

The contest came to a sudden end when all the fish were gone, and the Gulls stood once more as if the brawl had never happened. Max walked over to commend them, as would any true sportsman at the end of the game.

'Get lost,' came a response. 'You don't belong on our beach. Only a barbarian Magpie would steal fish from a civilized Seagull.'

Alice was surprised by the Seagull's rude attitude. It appeared that looking neat and acting civilized did not make them nice people. *Winners are grinners,* she thought. *Those bad losers can just stand there and sulk.*

They arrived at the end of the beach where Pete's rookery was only a short distance out. The flock flew there and waited for Pete to join them. The place appeared deserted but had a strong odour of bird toilet about it. Bernard asked Max a question. 'Do you think Pete lives here alone?'

'Why do you ask?' said Max.

'There appears to be a lot of poo about the place.'

'Perhaps Pete eats a lot of fish,' Max laughed.

Pete arrived, and Bernard asked him the question.

'No. Why would you ask that?' said a puzzled Pete.

Bernard laughed. 'I don't see anyone else claiming ownership to all this poo.' He liked joking at another's expense, but Pete's reaction was not what he expected.

'Thank you for the compliment,' said Pete, 'but I must confess that it has taken many generations of Penguins to give our island its unique charm.'

A Penguin chick heard Pete's voice and wandered out from under a rock. 'Hey Pete, when are my folks coming back. I'm hungry.'

Chicks began appearing from behind rocks and out of burrows. 'We are all hungry,' they cried.

'Settle down, kids,' said Pete. 'Sundown is your mealtime. Your parents will be back then.'

'I guess that answers Bernard's question,' Max chuckled.

Bernard laughed. 'All I can say is, well done Pete, and well done all you little Petes as well. You are doing an excellent job of turning this barren island into an exclusive retreat that any Penguin would enjoy.'

Bernard's weird sense of humour often caused embarrassment, but not to Pete. To him, Bernard could do no wrong, for Bernard was first to swoop the Seal, an action that had saved Pete's life.

That night, the flock roosted in the dunes. Max was excited, for he had found a Penguin, but Alice still had unanswered questions. Max found her perched in a bush, on her own, gazing into space. He asked her what was wrong.

'What is this wisdom and knowledge that I have come here to find,' she said. 'I have seen many things but now have more questions than before. I don't understand how the world can have no end to it. I don't understand how Humans can stand on water. In fact, I don't understand what wisdom and knowledge is.'

Max was not sure what to say. He was with her when Nebbie talked about wisdom and knowledge, but he never paid much attention to the subject. 'I think you have gained much wisdom,' he said, 'for you know what it is that you don't know.'

'Could you please repeat that,' Alice asked.

Max saw her puzzled look. 'Don't overthink things,' he said. 'You already have more wisdom and knowledge than any Magpie I know.'

49

A BAD PENNY

The flock left early the next morning, for Max was worried that the return journey would take longer. There would be no floating logs going their way, for the flow of the river would be against them. Grandma would have to fly, which meant having more rest breaks.

Max was also worried about the ground crew, wondering what fights they were having with no one to referee. They were two best friends who had argued since the day they first met. Only the fence between them had prevented an escalation to violence. Since joining the Road Runners, it had been Grandma's job to keep them under control. But with no fence and no Grandma, Max wondered what state his ground crew was now in.

The going was easy that first day because Mother Nature had summoned a tail wind to help them on their way. They were soon back to where the river flowed into the lake, but then Alice had a sudden thought. They had not seen the mouth of the river, but somehow, that no longer seemed to matter. She no longer wished to see the place where the sea drank Mother Nature's precious water, for she had seen Mother Nature wield her power over the waves. *If the sea was evil, Mother Nature would stop it from drinking the river,* she thought. *Perhaps I am gaining some wisdom and knowledge after all.*

The flock caught up with Grandma and the Cockatoos later that day, and Grandma was keen to get going while the wind was in their favour. By evening, they were back to where Trevor and Martha had camped, but the caravan was gone and so was Brian. Albert's heart sank. He had hoped that his favourite son would be there, but not so. Perhaps he would never see him again. Brian had put his trust in Humans above that of his family, but he would be at a loss once they tired of him.

'Brian has gone,' Albert lamented.

'Looks like it,' said Max, showing little concern for his brother.

Mayzie frowned. 'Max, you should be more worried about Brian. Look at your poor dad. He's heartbroken.'

'I doubt that we have seen the last of Brian,' laughed Max, for he regarded Brian's gone forever episodes as being only temporary. Brian always came back.

Charlie interrupted. 'I think Brian is a bad Penny.'

'What on earth are you talking about?' asked Max.

'I have studied Humans all my life,' said Charlie. 'They have a proverb which says, *a bad penny always turns up.* It means you can never get rid of someone because they keep coming back.'

'But what is a penny?' asked Max.

'Isn't that obvious?' said Charlie. 'It's the name of a bad girl called Penny.'

Max shrugged. 'I don't understand,' he said, 'but I agree that Brian will be back. Hopefully, he won't bring Penny with him.'

50

WHEN MOTHER NATURE CALLS

The wind came from a different direction the next morning and was no longer helping them. Max wondered if Mother Nature was punishing him for speaking unkindly about Brian. He thought about asking for Charlie's opinion but decided to ask Alice instead. He regarded Alice as wise, but someone needed to give her the confidence to realise it.

'Do you think Mother Nature is angry because I don't care about Brian?' he asked.

'I don't know,' said Alice, but then she thought some more. 'I will never have enough wisdom to understand what Mother Nature does, but I think she tries to be fair. She wouldn't punish us all for something only you have done.'

That makes sense, thought Max, for Grandma and the ground crew were the ones being punished, but he needed to do something about it. He asked Trailblazer if there was a shorter way back than having to follow the river.

'Not a problem,' said Trailblazer.

The flock set out, following Trailblazer across fields and trees before finding themselves back at the river. The shortcut had cut out several large bends.

Max recognised where they had come to, but the place now had a new feature. Music was coming from somewhere close. Once before, Max had heard music coming from the Church of Nowhere, and that was how he had met Lofty. Meeting Lofty had been a good thing, and he wondered if music was again guiding him toward someone special. 'We need to fly toward that music,' he told Trailblazer.

'That is not the shortest way home,' was the reply.

'I don't care,' said Max.

'Fine,' snorted Trailblazer. 'You're navigating for the rest of the day. I'm off for a short joy flight.'

Alice saw Trailblazer leave. 'Why is Trailblazer upset?' she asked.

'Trailblazer doesn't understand,' said Max. 'Mother Nature is not punishing us. She is using music to guide us to someone special.'

The flock began flying toward the music, but just when it seemed close, Grandma would have to rest. It would then fade into the distance.

Finally, Max realised that he needed a better plan, but that would require an apology to Trailblazer who had just returned. Max hated that part of the plan, but he had to know what was making the music. He apologised, and then asked Trailblazer for help.

'I already know what is making the music,' said Trailblazer.

'Tell me,' Max squawked.

'No,' said Trailblazer, 'I will let you find that out for yourself.'

Max was beginning to regret his apology, but then Trailblazer added, 'The music is travelling along the river, but I know a short cut we can use to head it off.'

'Lead on then,' said Max, and then he squawked, 'Ready Grandma?'

'Yes,' said Grandma in a feeble voice only a grandma can do. She was hoping that voice would cause Max to wait a little longer, but no such luck.

The flock flew across more fields and trees before re-joining the river again. 'Darn,' said Trailblazer. 'We missed it. It's just around the bend, but if we keep flying, we can catch it.'

Max looked down and saw churns in the water, and he wondered if the music was stirring the river. 'Keep going, everyone,' he squawked. 'We are nearly there.'

Grandma groaned. She was about ready to drop out of the sky, but she kept going. They rounded the bend, and to Grandma's relief, the music was a mystery no more. The paddleboat, which they had seen a few days earlier, was steaming upriver with music blaring from its windows.

'Do you think Mother Nature is in there?' laughed Alice.

'No, just Humans,' said a disappointed Max.

'Take a closer look on the roof,' said Trailblazer.

They looked and saw what Trailblazer had seen on his joy flight.

'Oh, good heavens,' said Alice.

The Humans are right about bad pennies, thought Charlie.

But Albert was ecstatic, and he squawked, 'Brian, my boy. It's me, your dad. It's good to see you again.'

Brian had taken possession of the paddleboat, or at least, that was how it seemed. He was perched on its roof. 'Come and join me,' he squawked. 'The Humans love having Magpies on board.'

'What about Cockatoos?' screeched Charlie.

'I'm sure they would love a pair of Cockatoos,' was the reply.

'What about a pair of Pigeons?' asked Trailblazer.

'Not sure about that,' Brian shouted. 'I heard the boat's engineer complaining about finding Pigeon poo on the deck.'

'That was probably Magpie poo,' laughed Bernard.

'No.' said Brian. 'He hasn't found where I hide that yet.'

Brian was at home on the roof of the paddleboat. The Humans all knew he was there and were giving him nice things to eat. He had found a place where he could happily spend the rest of his days.

Alice looked at Max and laughed. 'You were right, Maxie. Mother Nature has led us to someone special.'

Max had nothing to say.

Everyone, other than Grandma, landed bird like on the paddleboat. She came in with a flop and lay sprawled on its roof. Fortunately, there was no more flying for the day, for all were happy to stay where they were. That evening, the boat pulled into the bank where the crew moored it to a tree. With cruising suspended, the flock chose to roost on land that night, leaving the Humans to sleep on board.

Albert asked Brian the whereabouts of Trevor and Martha.

Brian shrugged. 'They went yesterday. They came on the boat for a day trip, and I followed. It was great. The passengers made a huge fuss of me, so I am going to stay on the boat forever.'

Albert's heart broke yet again, for it appeared that the reunion with his favourite son was destined to be short-lived.

51

CHAOS ON BOARD

The flock were having breakfast when a loud toot warned them that the boat was leaving. They flew back on board, but its engineer saw them return. He did not want birds on the boat and was already upset because the captain had allowed Brian to stay. It appeared that the captain followed a football team called the Magpies, which had earned Brian his special privilege. However, when the engineer told him that a flock of assorted birds had invaded the ship, the captain had to act. 'Best get rid of them, George,' he said. 'We can't have the passengers reporting vermin on the boat.'

The stowaways were on the roof, and they heard the captain's unkind remark. Charlie was shocked. 'Block your ears, Bella, my love. Surely, he can't be talking about us.'

But Charlie was wrong, for the engineer was soon on the roof, and he was waving a broom.

'Do you think he plans to fly away on that thing?' Bernard joked.

'I doubt it,' squawked Albert. 'I think he's out to get us.'

Bernard laughed. 'Perhaps he's looking for Brian's hidden stash of Magpie poo.'

Everyone beat a retreat to the foredeck, leaving the engineer on the roof with his broom. He cursed and resumed the chase. As he ran past the wheelhouse, he yelled, 'Don't worry, Captain, I will get them off the ship.' But his arrival on the foredeck saw the flock retreat once more to the roof. Again, he ran past the wheelhouse. This time, he heard the captain say, 'I think you need a better plan, George.'

The engineer was soon back on the roof, with the fire hose in his hand. He took aim and squirted, but his targets had already flown. The enemy was back on the foredeck.

'Gotcha this time,' yelled the engineer as a torrent of water splashed onto the foredeck, but everyone saw it coming. They headed for the shelter of the passengers' lounge, leaving the engineer to climb down from the roof. He ran past the wheelhouse once more and was rebuked by the captain.

'What are you trying to do, George, sink the ruddy ship? Turn off that fire hose.'

'Sorry, Captain.'

Suddenly, a scream came from the passengers' lounge. 'There's a Magpie in my porridge.'

Bernard looked at the screaming woman and wondered why his feet felt warm. Then he realised that he was standing in mush. He sampled a bit. *That tastes good,* he thought.

The Cockatoos landed on the bain-marie, where Charlie found a corncob on which to chew. He asked Bella to try one, and so she tramped through the scrambled eggs to join him. A passenger, who was thinking about having scrambled eggs, decided on the mushrooms instead.

The engineer came running through the door, armed with a tennis racquet.

'That's my tennis racquet,' yelled young Tommy who was one of the passengers.

'This tennis racquet has been commandeered to deal with an emergency,' yelled the engineer. He took a swipe at Penelope as she flew past.

'I wouldn't have him on my badminton team,' a passenger commented.

'Wait,' cried Tommy. 'You can't hurt those birds. I think they are the famous Road Runners.'

Everyone stopped and looked at Tommy, which gave Bernard another chance to sample the porridge. Meanwhile, Charlie had begun licking scrambled egg from Bella's feet.

'That looks better, my sweet,' said Charlie. 'I don't know why Humans leave things lying about where people can step in them.'

'Thank you, Charlie. You are such a dear.'

Young Tommy pulled out his smartphone. 'Look everybody, you can find them on YouTube.' He handed the phone to the engineer, but the engineer was not convinced.

'These birds are imposters,' he said. 'The Road Runners have a Sheep and Emu in their gang.' He waved the racquet in the air and yelled, 'Out of my lounge, vermin.'

The flock flew back to the roof with their accuser in hot pursuit. The captain shook his head as the engineer rushed past once more. *I have a feeling this is going to end badly,* thought the captain.

The engineer climbed back onto the roof, waving the tennis racquet above his head. He rushed at the flock but had forgotten about the fire hose he had dragged up there. He tripped, just managing to catch a glimpse of the captain's frown as he fell past the wheelhouse window.

I knew it, thought the captain. 'Man overboard,' he shouted as he turned the boat around.

The unwilling swimmer was hauled back on board, still clutching the tennis racquet. 'I'm going to get them,' he shivered.

'Let them go, George,' said the captain. 'They can have free passage on the roof. I don't think they will do any more harm provided you stop chasing them.'

'But, Captain.'

'That's an order, George. Go to your cabin and put on some dry clothes.'

The flock heard the captain's command and there were high-fives all round. They had free passage for the rest of the journey.

52

A FOND FAREWELL

The flock stayed on the boat for one more day. They thought their cruise would end when it reached the wall across the river, but not so. There was a chamber next to the wall with a gate at each end. The boat went through the first gate, stayed a while in the chamber, and then went through the second. It came out on the other side of the wall. Grandma was delighted. It appeared that their free ride was taking them all the way back to where they had left the ground crew.

Unfortunately, this was never going to happen because the ground crew was no longer where they had left them. Trailblazer was acting as lookout on the roof when everyone heard him coo, 'Ground crew on the starboard bow.'

Trailblazer could more easily have said, 'Look over there,' but he liked to put on a show. The fact was, he did not know his port from his starboard, but that did not matter, because no one else knew either. The captain could have told him he was wrong, but the captain had no idea what Trailblazer was cooing about.

Everyone looked to where Trailblazer pointed and saw the ground crew running beside the boat.

'Ahoy there, Garry and Lofty,' Max squawked. 'Take your time. We will meet you back at the bridge.' Max had not expected to find the ground crew so far down stream.

'I hurt my leg,' shouted Lofty.

Max sighed. 'It looks like we have to get off the boat. We need to see what is wrong with Lofty's leg.'

The flock abandoned ship and Brian went with them. The idea of being left on the boat with the crazy engineer did not appeal.

Young Tommy was enjoying lunch with the other passengers when he looked out and saw the Road Runners gathered on the bank. 'Look, everyone, they *are* the famous Road Runners,' he shouted. 'The Sheep and Emu are with them now.'

Tommy ran from the passengers' lounge and hung over the deck railing. 'Goodbye, Road Runners,' he yelled. 'It's been great to know you. Have a good life.' He began waving, and several passengers waved with him.

The engineer came on deck to investigate the shouting. 'See, they are all together now,' said Tommy. 'They are the famous Road Runners.'

'I still say they are vermin,' snorted the engineer as he stomped back to his engine room.

'Don't worry about him,' said one of the passengers. 'Only the famous Road Runners could do what everyone else wanted to do.'

'They threw the engineer overboard,' said a second passenger.

'That's right,' said the first. 'They mutinied.'

The Road Runners watched the paddleboat as it churned away from them, but they never knew that the captain was smiling as he looked back. The famous Road Runners had been on his boat and the double toot everyone heard, was the captain wishing them goodbye and good luck.

53

WHEN MITES BITE

Max asked the ground crew where they had been going.

'We were on a rescue mission,' said Garry.

'Who were you going to rescue?'

'You, of course. You were overdue, which meant you were in trouble. We were coming to your rescue.'

'How exactly were you going to perform this rescue?' Max laughed.

Garry shrugged, 'I don't know. I was leaving that part of the plan to Lofty.'

Alice looked at Lofty's leg. 'What happened there?' she asked.

'Can't remember.'

Then Alice noticed that Garry had a bloodshot eye. 'What happened to your eye?' she said.

'Can't remember.'

Alice took another look at Lofty's leg. 'Garry, that looks like teeth marks.'

'Does it? Lofty must have bitten himself.'

'Garry, Lofty has a beak, not teeth.'

'Oh, so he does.'

'Garry, did you and Lofty have a fight?'

'Maybe.'

'Over what?'

'Lofty poked me in the eye.'

'By accident?'

'Probably not.'

'Why then?'

'I can't help it if Lofty got all sensitive because I called him dopey.'

'Shame, Garry,' squawked Alice. 'One of my best friends is called Dopey. I think you deserved that poke in the eye.'

'You have a friend called Dopey,' said Garry, and then he rolled on the ground in laughter.

Max had to step in, for Garry was about to be swooped. 'I want no more fighting,' squawked Max, holding back his riled-up sister.

'You should all shake and be friends,' said Charlie.

Lofty began shaking his tail feathers.

'What good does shaking do?' Max asked.

'I don't know,' said Charlie, 'but Humans say it can prevent a fight.'

Max rolled his eyes. 'Lofty, you can stop shaking,' he said.

'Okay.'

The Road Runners camped by the bridge that night, where the ground crew hoped they would stay a few more days, but the flyers were keen to get back to Eden Springs. Everyone had begun to scratch, for the mites that once were Bella's, were now being shared by all.

Alice told them that Evelyn had a magic powder, which she sprinkled on the Chooks whenever they had mites. She called the powder her bug dust and it made the mites disappear.

Max had his doubts. He had long wrestled with the question, *are Humans good or bad people?* He thought most were bad, for they did things to displease Mother Nature. He also doubted that Evelyn had a magic powder, for only Mother Nature possessed magic. 'I don't think Humans know about magic,' he said.

Alice laughed. 'Do you remember when we were on the log, Maxie?'

'Yes.'

'Do you remember the two Humans that were chasing the boat?'

'Yes.'

'What else were they doing?

'Standing on the water.'

'I rest my case,' said Alice. 'You can stay here and scratch your feathers out, but I'm going back to be mended by Evelyn.'

'We're going back too,' shouted the others.

Max had no more to say, for he was yet to win an argument with his sister.

Charlie looked lovingly at Bella. 'You will soon have all your feathers back, my sweet. Your beauty will bloom once more.'

They arrived at Eden Springs two days later. Aunty Jenny, Horsie, and the Chooks, were there to welcome them.

'Where's Horatio?' asked Alice.

'Gone,' said Aunty Jenny. 'He said he was going back to the city where a Magpie of good character and breeding is appreciated'

'Good,' said Alice. 'He will make some poor girl a fine supervisor one day.'

Aunty Jenny agreed, but then she noticed the sorry state of their feathers. 'Oh dear, you all have mites,' she said. 'You will have to quarantine yourselves immediately.'

'Not by our chook house,' said the Chooks.

'And not by my stable,' said Horsie.

'I don't think Horses get bird mites,' said Alice.

'You don't know that for sure, and I'm taking no chances,' said Horsie. 'I suggest that you roost where the Crows sometimes perch.'

'That would be a bit mean,' said Alice. 'I don't want to give the Crows a reason to start another war.'

'Just a suggestion,' said Horsie, 'but don't stay here. You all need a dose of Evelyn's special powder.'

Alice looked at Max. 'See, Maxie, even Horsie knows about Evelyn's magic powder. Tomorrow, she will make our mites disappear.'

Max hoped that his sister was right, for his mites were yet to sleep. They made him itch both day and night. For the first time in his life, he had a problem that only a Human could fix, but he wondered if a Human would bother to perform such a miracle for a Magpie.

Evelyn woke next morning to the carolling of Magpies on her veranda. 'Colin, your Magpies are back,' she said. She looked out her front door. A chorus line of birds was perched to greet her, and all were scratching. 'Oh no,' she said. 'You lot are going nowhere until you have been fumigated. I'm getting my bug dust now.'

Max was alarmed. 'What does fumigate mean?' he asked Alice.

'Don't worry, Maxie, everything will work out fine.'

'But can we trust her? She said that we were Colin's Magpies. I'm not Colin's Magpie. I'm Max's Magpie.'

Alice frowned. 'Max, you have it all wrong. Colin doesn't own us. He sees us as part of his family. This is our home now. This is where we belong.'

Max had no choice. He would have to submit to being fumigated. He thought about the times he had accepted food from Humans. Such gestures could never make up for the crimes Humans committed against Mother Nature, but if Evelyn could banish his mites, he might be prepared to reconsider.

He lined up with the others and received a blessing of bug dust. The powder had an unpleasant odour, but to his mites, it was a weapon of mass destruction. The invaders were exterminated, and Max was delighted. Next day, Alice asked him, 'Have you changed your opinion about Humans now?'

Max said nothing. Evelyn and her family were indeed good Humans, but he had seen Humans do many bad things.

Max had become the most famous leader in Magpie history. He had met strange creatures from another world, observed things of interest to science, solved despicable crimes, and made a better life for his family and friends, but on the question of Humans being good or bad people, he had no answer.

Alice stared at him. 'Well?'

I don't know, he thought, but Alice deserved a better answer than that. Some time passed, and then he said, 'I think all Humans are different. Some are good, some are bad, and the rest are both. But the bad things Humans do spoils it for everyone. You have found good Humans here, but Mother Nature's creatures must always be on guard.'